The R

D1099365

iPods, iTunes
& Music Online

There are more than two hundred and fifty Rough Guide
travel, phrasebook and music titles, covering destinations
from Amsterdam to Zimbabwe, languages from Czech to
Vietnamese, and musics from World to Opera and Jazz

To find out more about Rough Guides,
and to check out our coverage of more than
10,000 destinations, find us on the Web at:

www.roughguides.com

Rough Guide Credits

Series editor: Mark Ellingham

Design and layout: Peter Buckley and Duncan Clark

Proofreading: Nikky Twyman

Production: Julia Bovis

Publishing Information

This first edition published October 2004 by
Rough Guides Ltd, 80 Strand, London WC2R 0RL,

375 Hudson Street, New York 10014
Email: *mail@roughguides.co.uk*

Distributed by the Penguin Group

Penguin Books Ltd, 80 Strand, London WC2R 0RL,
Penguin Putnam USA Inc., 375 Hudson Street, New York 10014, Penguin
Books Canada Ltd, 10 Alcorn Avenue, Toronto, Ontario MV4 1E4, Penguin
Books Australia Ltd,

PO Box 257, Ringwood, Victoria 3134,
Penguin Books (NZ) Ltd, 182–190 Wairau Road, Auckland 10

Printed in Spain by Graphy Cems

©Peter Buckley and Duncan Clark, 2004
224 pages; includes index

A catalogue record for this book is available
from the British Library

ISBN 1-84353-383-9

The Rough Guide to

iPods, iTunes
& Music Online

written by
Peter Buckley and Duncan Clark

ROUGH
GUIDES

Contents

Music online

More than music

Extras

Help & maintenance

iPodology

Introduction

why a book about iPods and iTunes?

When we first thought of writing this book, we wondered whether there would be enough to say. Apple are famous for making user-friendly products, and iPods and iTunes are particularly intuitive. But once we started chatting to people who either already had an iPod or were thinking of buying one, we realized there was clearly a need. Everyone had a question – "Is the sound quality any good?", "How do I move music between my two computers?", "AAC or MP3?", "Is downloading illegal?".

So here are a couple of hundred pages of answers, not only covering iPods and iTunes basics, but everything from finding music online and choosing the right audio file formats to resurrecting your old vinyl collection and getting it into your pocket. You'll also find a few samples of iPod culture – such as the devoted fans who obsess about their Pods' names and photograph the world reflected in their gadgets' mirrored backs. Not everyone is quite that keen, of course, but one thing that all Pod users agree on is that iPods change our relationship with music. And with the scores of tips and tricks provided in this little book, that relationship should be as satisfying as a Bach fugue. Or a Coltrane solo. Or a Missy Elliott acappella…

Note!

Each new version of iTunes brings a different set of features, and each new iPod model works slightly differently. This book was written using iTunes 4.5, so if you have something older, be sure to upgrade to the most recent version (see p.36) or many of the functions covered here will be missing. Likewise, if you have something newer (iTunes updates are released every few months), expect to find numerous extras.

As for hardware, this book focuses on the third-generation iPod and the new iPod Mini. Most of what we say will apply to older models, too, though certain features – Notes, Dock connectors, and so on – were only introduced with third-gen models.

BASICS &
BUYING

01

iPods &
digital music

everything you ever wanted
to know but were afraid to ask

This book should help you get the best from an iPod, from iTunes and from online music. However, before we get into the nitty-gritty of everything from ripping tracks from vinyl to using the iPod as a hard drive, let's address all those general questions that you've probably already asked yourself (and some that you probably haven't) about the world of MP3 players and digital music. You'll find more details on many of these subjects later on.

Basics

What is an iPod?

An iPod is like a cross between a Walkman and the hard drive used to store files in a computer. Instead of playing from cassettes, CDs or other media, it holds music internally as digital data, in just the same way as a computer stores word-processing documents, digital photos or any other files. iPods aren't unique in this respect: there are many devices that do roughly the same. They're collectively known as digital music players or (for reasons soon to be explained) MP3 players. But the

iPod – produced by Apple, best known for their Mac range of computers – is currently by far the most popular of the numerous brands on the market.

What's so good about digital music players?

There are numerous attractions to putting your music on an iPod or other high-spec digital music player. Compared to other types of personal stereo, they win hands down. For one thing, they can store a huge quantity of music – probably your entire CD collection many times over – so you can listen to whatever you want, wherever you are. Secondly, since there are no CDs or tapes to carry about, all you have to take with you is a small self-contained device, which, in the case of an iPod, is only around the size of a pack of playing cards. Furthermore, digital music players (like other personal stereos) can be hooked up to home hi-fis or car stereos, which means you have your entire music collection instantly accessible at home, at friends' houses, when you're driving – even on holiday.

Can they do anything else?

Besides being a record collection on the go, digital music players allow you to do numerous useful and interesting things. You can play tracks downloaded from the Internet, for example, without the hassle of burning a CD. You can instantly compile "playlists" of selected songs or albums: a four-hour upbeat selection for a party, say, or a shorter selection for a walk to work. Or have your player select your music for you, picking tracks randomly from across your whole collection or just from albums of a particular genre.

On top of all that, you can also use digital music players as portable hard drives to quickly back up or transfer any kind of computer files. A 40 GB iPod, for example, is the equivalent of roughly 30,000 floppy disks: enough to back up a huge quantity of documents, emails and photos. And most digital music players can also function as personal organisers – with electronic diaries, address books, musical alarm clocks, and so on – and even Dictaphones (see p.170).

Another good thing that digital music players can do is play audio books and other spoken-word recordings. Their large capacity makes it practical to store entire texts – so you don't have to make do with the hatchet-job abridgements typically found on cassettes and CDs.

Is an iPod the best digital music player to buy?

The various members of the iPod family are the best known digital music players and they have much to recommend them. They're solidly built but small and light. They're reliable and easy to use. They work with the excellent iTunes software (more on this below). There are scores of accessories and piles of extra software available for them. And they're masterpieces of ergonomic and aesthetic design. However, as with all Apple products, these qualities are reflected in the price.

There are many similar players which lack the wide reputation and slick design but which offer more features – such as an integrated radio, longer battery life, a bigger hard drive, the ability to record straight from a stereo rather than via a computer – for less money. Some even have mini video screens built in for viewing photos and movie clips (something expected to arrive on the next genereation of iPods).

There are also players designed to hold only a handful or a few dozen albums, as opposed to your whole collection. They store data on a microchip rather than a hard drive, and they are incomparably smaller and less expensive. They are so small, in fact, that they are sometimes integrated into a pair of headphones or designed to live on a keyring.

MP3 players like this one use a chip rather than a hard drive. They are smaller, cheaper and much lower capacity than iPod-style, hard-drive-based players

To get a sense of how iPods compare to other digital music players on the market, browse the selection and customer reviews at www.amazon.com or www.amazon.co.uk.

I've heard the sound quality isn't great. Is that true?

Audiophiles sometimes turn their noses up at iPods and other digital music players on the grounds that the sound quality is not too hot. It's true that – at the default settings – the sound is marginally worse than CD, but you're unlikely to notice much (or any) difference unless you do a careful side-by-side comparison through a decent home stereo. Anyway, this sound quality isn't fixed. When you import tracks from CD (or record them from vinyl) you can choose from a wide range of options, up to and including full CD quality. The only problem is that better-quality recordings take up more disk space, which means fewer tracks on your iPod. Still, the trade-off between quality and quantity is entirely for you to decide upon. For more on this, see p.106.

Can an iPod really hold my whole CD collection?

That depends on the model you buy, the sound quality you desire and – obviously – the size of your collection. The top-of-the-range iPod at the time of writing is capable of storing around 1000 albums at a sound quality that will satisfy most people: that's enough music to play day and night for nearly a whole month without a single note repeating. So, assuming you own less music than that, you don't insist on super-high fidelity, and you're prepared to pay for a suitably capacious model, then yes, an iPod can hold your whole music collection. However, it's worth bearing in mind that in practice you also need the same

basics & buying

Computer requirements & upgrade options

Any Mac or PC produced in the last few years, including laptops, should be fine for use with an iPod, and many older ones will also work. But it's certainly worth checking your hardware before buying a Pod. The core requirements are a recent operating system and the right socket to plug the iPod into. But you'll also need enough hard drive space to store your music. A fast Internet connection also helps. Let's look at these four requirements in turn.

▶ **Windows XP (or 2000) or Mac OS X.** To check what operating system you have on a PC, right-click the My Computer icon and select Properties. If you have Windows Me or 98, you could consider upgrading to XP but you'll have to pay (around £85/$95); it can be a bit of a headache (some older programs and hardware don't work on XP); and you'll need to check whether your hardware is up to the job. If you have Windows 95, it's probably a matter of buying a new computer. Windows 2000 users should be OK, though will need to make sure they have downloaded the latest updates from Microsoft via Windows Update in the Start menu.

On a Mac, select About This Mac or System Profiler from the Apple menu. If you have any version of OS X you'll be OK, though you might have to run the Software Update tool to grab the latest version. If you have OS 9 or earlier, you could upgrade to the latest version of OS X for around £90/$130. Your old applications should all continue to work in "Classic Mode".

▶ **A FireWire or USB2 socket.** This is the "port" needed to connect an iPod. The ideal option is a FireWire port (also known by the more prosaic title of **IEEE1394**), which you'll find on all Macs produced in the last five or so years and most recent PCs. Almost as good is a USB2 socket, found on many PCs and Macs made after 2002, though currently only the iPod Minis come with a USB2 wire included. Check your manual to see which sockets you have: it's hard to tell by looking, as USB2 sockets look identical to standard USB.

If you don't have FireWire or USB2, you could attach your iPod via a standard USB socket, though this will make transferring music and other files between computer and iPod around ten times slower. Alternatively, you could add a FireWire or USB2 port with the suitable add-on card. These are available for as little as £20/$30 for desktops and around double that for laptops. If you do have the right port but it's already occupied by another device, you could either plug and unplug the deivces according to what you're using at any one time or buy a "hub" to turn a single port into multiple ports. These start at around £30/$50.

▶ **Lots of hard drive space**. You ideally need at least as much free hard drive space as the size of the iPod you're planning on buying (and probably more if you're buying a small-capacity model). To find out how big and how full your hard drive is on a PC, open My Computer, right-click the C-drive icon and select properties; on a Mac, single-click your hard drive icon on the Desktop or in a Finder window and select Get Info from the File menu. If you don't have enough space – bearing in mind that you can fit around fifteen to twenty albums on one gigabyte – try deleting any large files that you no longer need (or burning them to CDs) and then empty the Recyling Bin or Trash. On a PC, you could also try running the Disk Cleanup utility: right-click the C-drive icon, select Properties, and then press the Disk Cleanup button. If you still don't have enough space, consider adding an extra hard drive to your computer: these start at around £30/$50 for one that can be installed inside your computer's body, with higher-capacity and external drives (necessary for laptops) costing more.

▶ **An Internet connection**. You can survive without this, but an Internet connection allows you to do clever things such as automatically add the track and artist names for all the music you copy from CD. It also allows you to download tracks from the Internet, though this can be frustratingly slow unless you have a broadband connection.

For everything you need to know about choosing, using and upgrading a PC or Internet connection, see this book's sister volumes: *The Rough Guide to PCs & Windows* and *The Rough Guide to the Internet*.

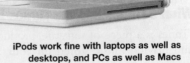

iPods work fine with laptops as well as desktops, and PCs as well as Macs

amount of space available on the hard drive of your computer, since whatever is on your iPod will typically also live on your PC or Mac.

So I need a computer, too?

Yes – or at the very least you need access to one. For one thing, a computer is the only way to get music onto an iPod. To copy a CD onto it, for example, you first copy it onto the computer (you "rip" the CD, to use the jargon) and then transfer it from the computer to the iPod. You can't cut out this step because the iPod has neither a CD drive nor the necessary processing power to extract the music directly. But even if you could cut out this step, it would still be better to combine your iPod with a computer: that way, you don't lose all your music if your iPod is lost, broken or stolen. And a computer also allows you to download music from the Internet.

Is my current computer up to the job?

If you bought a PC or Mac in the last few years, it will probably be capable of working with an iPod, but it's certainly worth checking before blowing all your money. The box on the previous page explains the minimum requirements and the upgrade options if your computer doesn't have what it takes.

What's iTunes and the iTunes Music Store?

iTunes is a piece of software, produced by Apple, for managing and playing music stored on your computer. It's also used for moving music from your computer to your iPod, but you don't need an iPod to use iTunes. If you're mainly interested in creating a digital music collection to listen to at home – rather than carry around with you – you can do this using iTunes. After all, your computer can do everything an iPod can do, including being hooked up to a hi-fi (see p.119).

Another function of iTunes is to provide access to the iTunes Music Store, which is one of various Internet-based services from which you can legally buy and download music. This is currently the *only* way to access the Store: you can't shop there by visiting the Apple website using a regular Web browser. Note, though, that you don't have to buy music from the iTunes Music Store. You can use iTunes to play music copied from CD or other computers, or downloaded from elsewhere on the Internet (though music files from certain other online music stores may not be compatible).

There are many other programs similar to iTunes (but without the built-in iTunes Music Store access). They're collectively referred to as "jukeboxes". Though it is possible to use the iPod with a different jukebox program (see p.184), there's currently not that much reason why you'd want to.

OK. Sounds good. But...

Isn't copying and downloading music illegal?

No. The only thing that's illegal is taking copyrighted material that you haven't acquired legitimately – and, of course, distributing copyrighted material that you have acquired legitimately. In short, you're well within your rights to copy your own music collection onto your computer and iPod, as long as you don't then copy the files onto your friends' computers or iPods. As for music on the Internet, there are numerous legal options, including online services that sell individual tracks to download and keep, and others which offer unlimited access to a music archive in return for a monthly fee. There's also plenty of downloadable music that's both legal and free: one-off promotions from major labels, for example, and songs by little-known musicians more interested in establishing their name than making a profit.

However, it's true that, at the present, the majority of music downloaded from the Internet is copyrighted material taken for free from file-sharing networks such as KaZaA. Though you are relatively unlikely to get prosecuted for taking part in this free-for-all, it is definitely illegal. For the full lowdown on downloading, see p.127.

What if my computer dies?

Hard drives occasionally just crash, in which case the only potential option for getting the contents back is a very expensive data-recovery process. And, of course, computers meet many other nasty ends: theft, lightning, spilled coffee and so on. If this happens, and you lose all the music stored on your PC or Mac's hard drive, it can be a real pain. However, with a little know-how (see p.182) it's possible to move all your music back from your iPod onto a new hard drive or computer (Apple tend to keep this relatively quiet, since it makes it very easy to illegally distribute your music collection onto your friends' computers). Obviously, however, you'll only be able to transfer what's on the iPod at that time, so if you don't keep your entire collection on both your computer and your iPod, it's definitely worth backing up your hard drive (see p.189).

What was that furore in the press about iPod batteries?

The current generation of iPods have rechargeable, lithium-ion batteries, much like the ones in laptop computers. They last up to around eight hours after a two- or three-hour charge but, like all such batteries, they don't live forever. After a couple of years of heavy use or a longer period of light use, they start holding less and less power and eventually die. When iPod users first realized this, they were shocked to learn that the battery was not user-replaceable and that to have it replaced by Apple would cost so much that they may as well bin the iPod and buy a new one.

After much public pressure and a few legal threats, Apple dropped the price of the service to $99 in the US, and an equivalent amount elsewhere (still a lot, though no more than an average laptop battery). Since then, various third-party services have popped up offering a much cheaper "unofficial" service. If you look online, you'll also find instructions for doing it yourself. For more info, see p.196.

The Neistat Bros were so upset when they realized their iPod batteries were effectively non-replaceable that they felt obliged to make a film. Happily, the batteries can now be replaced for much less than the price of a new iPod.

Isn't it a hassle to transfer all my music from CD to computer to iPod?

It certainly takes a while to transfer a large CD collection onto your computer, but not as long as it would take to play the CDs. Depending on your computer, it can take just a few minutes to transfer the contents of a CD onto your computer's hard drive – and you can listen to the music, or do some work in another application, while this is happening. Still, if you have more money than time, there are services that will take away your CDs and rip your collection for you (www.podserve.co.uk).

Once the music is on your PC or Mac, it only takes ten minutes or so to transfer a whole large collection across to the iPod; and subsequent transfers from computer to iPod are even quicker, as only new or changed files can be copied over.

Isn't this whole thing just another consumerist fad from a money-grabbing music industry?

The extraordinary range of music formats we've had in the last half century – vinyl, cassette, CD, DAT, MiniDisc, SACD – has often been described as a cynical ploy by the music and electronics industries to make us buy ever more equipment and multiple copies of the same recordings. Whatever your view on this, digital music players such as the iPod are qualitatively different from the rest. For a start, they certainly weren't dreamed up by the music industry: in fact, the music industry is quaking in its boots about anything that combines music with computers, since the world of "digital music" makes it incredibly easy to illegally share copyrighted material – both via the Internet or simply by copying, say, 500 albums from a friend in a matter of minutes.

As for whether iPods are another unnecessary consumer fad from the electronics industry is a matter for debate. True, they're ultimately expensive gadgets bought and designed by wealthy Westerners and manufactured in an oppressive regime where labour rights are poor (China). The same is true for much electronic equipment. But from an environmental perspective, at least, you can make a pretty strong case for a device that deals with music purely as digital data: downloading, compared to buying CDs, means no more delivery trucks and no more unnecessary packaging. An iPod, after all, only weighs as much as two boxed CDs, but holds the same amount of music as 1000.

What's DRM?

As we've already seen, there's nothing the record industry fears more – understandably enough – than the uncontrolled distribution of its copyrighted music. It's hard to see how the record companies will be able to stop people sharing files that they have copied from their own CDs, even if they succeed in killing off file-sharing networks like KaZaA (see p.143). However, the labels – and online music retailers – do have a strategy for stopping people freely distributing tracks that they've purchased and downloaded from legitimate online music stores. It's called DRM – digital rights management – and it involves embedding special code into music files to impose certain restrictions on what you can do with them. For example, music downloaded from the iTunes Music Store has embedded DRM which stops you from making the tracks available on more than a certain number of computers at one time (for details, see p.134). Other online services, meanwhile, use DRM to stop you burning downloaded files to CD.

Is that an infringement of my rights?

This is a hotly debated issue. Advocates of free distribution of music see DRM as an infringement of their rights, while others see it as a legitimate way for record labels and retailers to safeguard their products from piracy. So Apple's adoption of the technology has elicited a mixed response. But the DRM debate is really just one part of a bigger argument about whether it's ethical to "share" copyrighted music. The sharers claim that music is about art not money; that most of the artists being downloaded are already millionaires; that sharing is a great way to experience new music (some of which you might then buy on CD); and that if the record industry really is in trouble, they deserve it for ripping off consumers with overpriced albums for so many years. The industry, on the other hand, says that sharing – or theft, as they prefer to put it – deprives artists of royalties and record labels of the money they need to produce new albums. The result, they claim, will be fewer musicians and less new music in the future.

What about all my CDs?

Unless you're a sound-quality connoisseur or a fan of sleeve notes, you might find that once your music collection has been copied onto your computer and iPod, the original CDs start to seem like a waste of space. Some have advocated selling them: after all, many CDs will go for £5/$10 through online auctions such as eBay, so if you sell enough you can end up far better off than before you bought your iPod. Strictly speaking, though, this is legally dodgy. You should delete the music from your iPod and computer the moment you sell the CD, since you are no longer the rightful owner of the music.

Getting technical

How is the music stored?

Clever though computers are, they only deal with numbers: digital, rather than analogue, information. In fact, their vocabulary is limited to just zeros and ones: the "binary" number system. So music on a computer or iPod – whether it's a folk song or a symphony – is reduced to a series of millions of zeros or ones. Or, more accurately, it's reduced a series of tiny magnetic or electronic charges, each representing a zero or a one. A typical song would consist of around 30 million zeros and ones, while a full 40 GB iPod holds around 300 billion zeros and ones – roughly 50 for every person on the planet.

But aren't CDs also "digital"?

Absolutely. The idea of reducing music to zeros and ones is nothing new: CDs, MiniDiscs and any other "digital" music formats also store music as zeros and ones. But none of these other formats combine the capacity, flexibility and editability of the hard drive in an iPod.

I've heard of MP3s. But what are they exactly?

Computers store information – such as documents, spreadsheets and images – as "files", and there are various different formats for each kind of file. A fancy text document created in Microsoft Word, for example, is saved in the "doc" format, while a simpler text-only document with no fancy styling is usually saved as a "txt" file. Likewise, a professional-quality photo might be in the tiff format, while the same image displayed on a website would probably be a JPEG, which looks very nearly as good but is incomparably quicker to download. The format is usually included in a file's name – Memo.doc or John.jpg, for example.

Music on computers and iPods can be stored in numerous file formats, but the ones you need to know about are the ubiquitous MP3 (or Moving Pictures Experts Group-1/2 Audio Layer 3 to give it its rather grandiose full title) and the more recent AAC (Advanced Audio Coding). Like JPEGs for images, these are formats designed for squeezing lots of information into very small files; in fact, technically speaking the names MP3 and AAC refer not just to the file format but also to the "compression algorithms" used to do the squeezing. Each format has its pros and cons (see p.105), but they both achieve pretty amazing feats of compression. When a computer turns the uncompressed audio information on a CD into MP3 or AAC, the resulting file sounds almost identical to the original but is around ninety percent smaller. That means ten times as much music on your iPod and ten times quicker downloads from the Internet.

This compression is achieved through a remarkable combination of mathematics and psychoacoustics: the algorithms are clever enough to take out what your brain does not process (the vast majority of the sound) and leave the rest untouched. For a full explanation, see **www.mp3-converter.com/mp3codec**

Amazing. But my vinyl-junkie friends tell me that CDs are also compressed. Is that true?

Technically speaking, yes, any digital recording could be described as being compressed, since taking the infinitely rich and varied analogue sounds of the real world and turning them into a finite series of numbers inevitably involves losing something. Indeed, many people prefer vinyl (which isn't digital) to CDs for just this reason: they claim it sounds richer and more real. But that's a separate discussion. The point here is that, in the context of iPods, MP3s and the like, compression refers to the compressing of digital files into smaller digital files, not the compression of the musicians into numbers.

Each individual track can be compressed to a greater or lesser extent. This is measured in bitrates.

What's a bitrate?

The bitrate of a digital music file is the amount of data (the number of "bits", or zeros and ones) that is used to encode each second of music. This is measured in Kbps: kilo (thousand) bits per second. (Incidentally, if you've ever heard of a "56k modem", the k in that context means exactly the same thing: the number of bits transferred per second.) Most music online, on computers and in iPods is encoded at a bitrate of 128, 160 or 192 kbps, which means that each second of sound is made up of around 100,000 to 200,000 zeros and ones. However, higher and lower bitrates are not uncommon, especially for spoken-word recordings, where the sound quality is not quite so important.

How big is a gig?

The storage capacity of iPods, like other hard drives, is measured in gigabytes – also called gigs or GBs. Roughly speaking, a byte is eight zeros and ones (the space required on a computer disk to store a single character of text), and a gigabyte is one billion bytes. Or, to compare to other file sizes that you may have come across, a gig is the same as 1000 MB (megabytes), which is also the same as 1,000,000 KB (kilobytes).

Mathematically minded readers may be interested to know that all these figures are actually approximations of the number two raised to different powers. A gigabyte is two bytes to the power of thirty, which equals 1,073,741,824 bytes.

02 Buying an iPod

which model? where from?

There are a number of different models of iPod. They all have essentially the same capabilities, the main variables being physical size, the capacity of the hard drive and, of course, price. However, different models also come with different accessories thrown in. The following few pages should help you chose which iPod is most suitable for your needs. You'll also find tips on how to shop for the best deal and some pointers to websites worth browsing before you buy.

Standard iPod (lifesize)

iPod Mini (lifesize)

basics & buying

What to buy

At the time of writing, iPods come in two types: standard and mini. The standard ones all look pretty much the same (give or take a millimetre or two of depth) but have different sizes of hard drive. Conversely, the minis come in various different colours, but are all the same inside. The table opposite shows you how much music – or spoken word – each model can hold, while the lifesize pictures on pp. 22 and 23 show you the comparative sizes.

You don't necessarily need an iPod with a hard drive capable of holding your whole music collection – or even as big as the collection you intend to digitize. You can store your whole collection on your computer's hard drive and just copy across to your iPod the albums you want to listen to at any one time. That, of course, relies on you having enough space on your computer's hard drive (to find out how to check, see p.9).

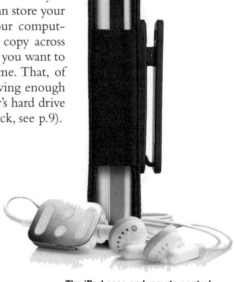

The iPod case and remote control are included with some models.

Which model?

Following are some details, including their music capacity, on the various iPod models available at the time of writing (summer 2004). To find the latest specs, prices and bundled extras, visit www.apple.com

MODEL:	Mini (4 GB)	15 GB	20 GB	40 GB
CAPACITY				
Songs at 128 Kbps (high-quality)	1000	3700	5000	10,000
Songs at 160 Kbps (extra-high quality)	800	3000	4000	8000
Songs at 192 Kbps (audiophile quality)	650	2000	3300	6700
Hours at 32 Kbps (for spoken word)	270	1000	1350	2700
SIZE				
Body (inches)	3.6x2.0x0.5	4.1x2.4x0.6		4.1x2.4x0.73
Body (mm)	91.5x50.8x12.7	104x61x15.2		104x61x18.5
Screen (diagonal in inches)	1.67	2		2
WEIGHT				
In ounces	3.6	5.6		6.2
In grams	104	158		176
INCLUDED				
Dock	✗	✗	✓	✓
Remote control	✗	✗	✓	✓
USB2 lead	✓	✗	✗	✗
FireWire lead	✓	✓	✓	✓

One thing worth bearing in mind when choosing how many gigs you need is that if you plan to use the iPod as a portable hard drive (see p.155) as well as a digital music player, you'll need some extra space available. Also note that the "actual" formatted capacity of an iPod (like all hard drives) is more than five percent smaller than advertised. So a 40 GB model is really around 37.5 gigs, and a 4 GB model around 3.75 gigs.

The other main consideration are the accessories thrown in. The difference in price between the least expensive standard model and the next one up seems relatively small when you factor in extras such as a dock and remote control. You can manage without either, but the dock is very convenient – especially if you use your iPod through your home stereo – and the remote control (which becomes part of the headphone cable) saves you digging the iPod out of your pocket every time you want to change the volume or skip a track.

Where to buy

As with all Apple products, they cost basically the same amount no matter where you buy them. The price you'll get direct from Apple...

Apple Store US www.apple.com/store ▸ 1-800-MY-APPLE
Apple Store UK www.apple.com/ukstore ▸ 0800-039-1010

...will typically be only a few pounds/dollars more (or occasionally less) than the price you'll find from the many other dealers on that sell online or on the high street. That said, different sellers may throw in different extras, from engraving on the back of the iPod to a pair of portable speakers. In the US market you can keep track of these various offers and discounts at the brilliant "Buyers' Guides" section of:

Mac Review Zone www.macreviewzone.com

Or try a price-comparison agent such as:

Froogle www.froogle.com
PriceWatch www.pricewatch.com
Shopper.com www.shopper.com
Shopping.com www.shopping.com

In the UK, price-comparison agent includes:

Kelkoo www.kelkoo.co.uk
Shopping.com uk.shopping.com

Buying from a "real" high-street store typically means paying the full standard price, but you'll get the iPod immediately. If you order over the phone or Internet from Apple, you can expect up to a week's wait for delivery. For a list of dealers in the UK, follow the link from www.apple.com/uk/hardware. In the US (and London), you can go straight to one of Apple's own high-street stores. For a list, see:

Apple Stores www.apple.com/retail

That said, some online retailers tend to be much quicker, including the best known of all:

Amazon US www.amazon.com
Amazon UK www.amazon.co.uk

Refurbished iPods

Apple, and a few retailers, offer refurbished iPods. These are either end-of-line models or up-to-date ones which have been returned for some reason. They come "as new" – checked, repackaged and with a full standard warranty – but they are reduced in price by up to 40 percent (usually more like 15 percent). The only problem is availability: the products are in such hot demand that, in the UK, you can only see Apple's selection on Wednesdays, from 10am onwards (get there early).

Apple Store UK Refurbished
http://promo.euro.apple.com/promo/refurb/uk

In the US, supply is also limited, though you can at least check whether anything is on offer throughout the week. Follow the Special Deals link from the Apple Store website (www.apple.com/store) or, for the most up-to-date information about availability, call 1-800-MY-APPLE. Alternatively, check with your local Apple retailer to see whether they offer refurbished or returned iPods.

Secondhand iPods

Buying a secondhand iPod is much like buying any other piece of used electronic equipment: you might find a bargain but you might land yourself with an overpriced bookend. That said, the standard Apple warranty is international and, in practice at least, transferable, so if you buy one that is less than a year old (and with the documentation to prove it) you should be able to get it repaired for free if anything goes wrong inside. Obviously, that will rely on the type of damage being covered by the warranty.

Whatever you buy, make sure you see it in action before parting with any cash, but remember that this won't tell you everything. If an iPod's been used a lot, for example, the battery might be on its last legs and soon need replacing, which will add substantially to the cost (see p.196). Also remember that older models won't necessarily support more recent accessories or software.

Laser engraving

If you purchase from Apple, you'll be offered the chance to have a message, name, slogan or whatever typographic message you like laser-engraved on the iPod's shiny backside. This is the iPod equivalent of a tattoo, so think very carefully as you're stuck with it. If you want a few ideas, to create a virtual engraving to see what it would look like, or just to laugh at some of the best and worst engravings ever requested, visit:

iPod Laughs www.ipodlaughs.com/ipod/iengraver
Methodshop www.methodshop.com/mp3/articles/ipodengraving

> **TIP: Consider getting your name and either an email address or telephone number engraved on your iPod; at least this gives it a fighting chance of finding its way back to you if lost; and, if stolen, the thief will have a hard time selling it on.**

To buy or to wait?

When shopping for any piece of computer equipment, there's always the tricky question of whether to buy the current model, which may have been around for a few months, or hang on for the next version, which may be both better and less expensive. In the case of iPods, the situation is worse than normal, both because they're not inexpensive and because Apple are famously secretive about their plans to release new or upgraded versions of their hardware.

Unless you have a friend who works in Apple HQ – and an opportunity to get them drunk – you're unlikely to hear anything from the horse's mouth about new iPod models until the day they appear. So, unless a new model came out recently, there's always the possibility that your new purchase will be out of date within a few weeks. About the best you can do is check out some sites where rumours of new models are discussed. But don't believe everything you read…

Apple Insider www.appleinsider.com
Mac Rumors www.macrumors.com
Think Secret www.thinksecret.com

USING iTUNES
& THE iPOD

03
iTunes
quickstart

a whistlestop intro to iTunes

Before diving into advanced functions and settings, file formats, software add-ons, accessories and the rest, let's take a quick spin around iTunes, get everything up and running, rip a few tunes from a CD onto your computer, and get them onto your iPod. Even if you've been using a Pod for years, it's probably worth browsing through this section, as even some of the basic iTunes functions are easy enough to miss – and we've included plenty of tips and tricks.

iTunes – your first time

If you are using a Mac running OS X, iTunes will already be on your machine and will, by default, appear on the Dock. If it's not on the Dock, look in your Applications folder. If it's not there either, or you're using a PC, you'll need to install it from the CD that came with your iPod: just slot it into the computer and, if nothing happens automatically, look for the iTunes folder.

The installation process itself is pretty self-explanatory on the Mac, but on a PC the "Wizard" is a little more clunky and can take some time (for one thing, you'll be asked to enter your iPod's serial number, which can be found in almost indecipherable small print on the gadget's mirrored backside). The "InstallShield Wizard" not only installs iTunes on the PC, but also the necessary drivers to run your iPod through Windows.

Once it's installed, you'll find the iTunes icon – a CD and a couple of musical notes – on your Dock (Mac) or the Start Menu and Quick Launch area (PC). Double-click it to launch the program. Since this is the first time you are using iTunes, the Setup Assistant Wizard will appear on-screen, prompting you to make a few decisions, probably including the following (you can also change these settings later in the iTunes Preferences panel):

▶ Yes, use iTunes for Internet audio content or
▶ No, do not alter my Internet settings

This is asking whether you'd like your computer to use iTunes (as opposed to whatever plug-ins you are currently using) as the program to handle sound and files such as MP3s when surfing the Web. iTunes can do a pretty good job of dealing with online audio, but if you'd rather stick with your existing Internet audio setup, hit "No".

▶ Yes, automatically connect to the Internet or
▶ No, ask me before connecting

iTunes will sometimes want to access the Internet (for example, to find track names for you or access the iTunes Music Store). If you use a standard dial-up Internet connection you probably should select "No" – this way you won't accidentally block your phoneline or spend extra money (if you pay per minute for access). If you have broadband, click "Yes".

▶ Do you want to search for music files on your computer and copy them to the iTunes library?

Unless you have music files scattered around your computer, and you'd like them automatically put in one place, select "No", otherwise you might end up with non-music sound files in your music library. You can always add music – automatically or manually – later.

▶ Do you want to go straight to the iTunes Music Store?

Decline the invitation for now. For information about downloading from the Apple Store and elsewhere, see p.129.

After all this you should be presented with the main iTunes window…

using iTunes & the iPod

The iTunes environment

The iTunes application doubles as both a media player for your computer and an interface for your iPod, and some of the controls and buttons will differ depending on whether your Pod is connected. But, in its virgin state, the iTunes environment consists of the following.

Get the latest version

Before getting too comfortable with all the ins and outs of your newly installed copy of iTunes, go online and make sure you're running the latest version. You may be prompted to do this automatically, but you can also do it manually at any time. On a Mac, click "Software Update" from the Apple menu; if a new version of iTunes (or the iPod software) is available, it will appear in the list. On a PC, open iTunes and select from Check For iTunes Updates from the Help menu.

Along the top...

Below the application's main menus are, starting from the left, the primary play controls and volume slider, which works independent of your computer's master volume control. Then, in the middle, there's the "status" area, which displays info about the track currently playing or importing and, when you click the small triangular icon on its left, becomes an attractive but fairly worthless EQ display.

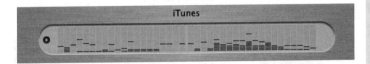

Next up is the Search field: type into it to find tracks in your iTunes music library. The dropdown menu next to the magnifying glass icon allows you to choose exactly how you want to search – by artist, album, song, etc. Finally, there's the circular button on the right, which, again, alters its function depending on what you are doing. When viewing your music library it toggles the browse function on and off (see p.47); when a CD is present it prompts you to "Import" the tracks (see p.44); and when a playlist is selected it gives you the option to burn a CD from that playlist (see p.90).

The Source list

Situated on the left, the Source list is the doorway to your music files (via the Library icon and playlists), Internet radio stations (see p.149), other people's shared music (see p.149) and the iTunes Music Store (see p.129). When connected, this list also features an icon for your iPod as well as any music CDs that are currently in your machine.

using iTunes & the iPod

The song list

The big striped panel that accounts for the majority of the iTunes window lists the songs within whichever source is selected in the source list. The tracks displayed can be sorted alphabetically or numerically according to any of the various columns of information – click on the top of a column to sort by it. Though the song list seems at first to be an element of iTunes that needs little elaboration, there are various ways to customize it; see p.82 to find out more.

	Song Name	Artist	Time	Album
1	☑ Sinfonia 10 in G major BWV 796	Glenn Gould	0:57	Bach: Inventions and Sinfonias
2	☑ Sonata 28 in A major, Op 101: IV. ...	Maurizio Pollini	7:33	Beethoven: The Late Piano Sonatas (Disc 1)
3	☑ Six Little Piano Pieces, Op. 19: V. E...	Maurizio Pollini	0:35	Schoenberg & Webern Piano Music
4	☑ No. 13 in F# Major. Prelude	Glenn Gould	2:17	Bach: Well-Tempered Clavier I (Disc 2)
5	☑ Sonata in B minor, Kk 87	Clara Haskil	4:35	Scarlatti: 11 Sonatas
6	☑ Variation 6 – Allegro ma non tropp...	Piotr Anderszewski	1:56	Beethoven: Diabelli Variations
7	☑ Invention 14 in B-flat major BWV 7...	Glenn Gould	1:37	Bach: Inventions and Sinfonias
8	☑ Piano Sonata No.31: III	Piotr Anderszewski	1:40	Bach, Beethoven and Webern Recital
9	☑ Six Little Piano Pieces, Op. 19: III. S...	Maurizio Pollini	1:01	Schoenberg & Webern Piano Music
10	☑ No. 23 in B Major. Fugue	Glenn Gould	1:36	Bach: Well-Tempered Clavier I (Disc 2)
11	☑ English Suite No. 6: VII. Gavotte II–...	Piotr Anderszewski	2:12	Bach, Beethoven and Webern Recital
12	☑ No. 15 in G Major. Fugue	Glenn Gould	2:22	Bach: Well-Tempered Clavier I (Disc 2)
13	☑ Ballata no. 1 op 23 in sol minore	Arturo Benedetti Michelangeli	9:17	Chopin Recital, Vatican, 1986
14	☑ No. 14 in F# Minor. Fugue	Glenn Gould	3:51	Bach: Well-Tempered Clavier I (Disc 2)
15	☑ Sonata in E flat major, Kk 193	Clara Haskil	4:08	Scarlatti: 11 Sonatas
16	☑ Invention 2 in C minor BWV 773	Glenn Gould	2:54	Bach: Inventions and Sinfonias
17	☑ Andante spianato e grande polacca...	Arturo Benedetti Michelangeli	13:03	Chopin Recital, Vatican, 1986

> **TIP: Click and drag the thin silver-grey strip between the source list and song list to adjust the relative size of the two panels.**

And along the bottom...

To the left there are four buttons. The first adds a new, untitled playlist to the source list (see p.63 for more on playlists). The second activates the shuffle playback mode (which is also called "random", though you may find it seems distinctly un-random;

see p.69). When the third button with the looping arrows is clicked and becomes

illuminated, whichever source is currently in use (be it a CD, a playlist or your whole library) will play on cycle ad infinitum. Another click of the same button adds a circled "1" to the icon, which means iTunes will now loop only the individual song. The final button opens a frame at the bottom of the source list where an image can be placed for that track – the album cover art, for example (see p.85).

On the right there are three more buttons. The first unleashes the iTunes Equalizer window (see p.114), the second turns on

the iTunes Visualizer (see p.71), and the third ejects CDs. Once you start stocking your iTunes Library the lower strip will also start to display useful data in its centre, telling you – for whichever source or playlist that's currently selected – the number of songs present, the total playing time and, most usefully, the total file size the songs collectively take up. This is handy when building playlists to burn to CD, and also offers a means of checking exactly how much of your computer's hard drive is being taken up by your collection: to get the bottom line, click the Library icon in the source list and check the stats.

2241 songs, 6.3 days, 8.89 GB

> **TIP:** The total playing time displayed at the bottom of the iTunes window is approximate; click the displayed time and it will change to an exact reading.

Ripping a CD

The best way to get your head around iTunes is to plant some music in it and start playing. Let's start by copying some tracks from a CD to your computer's hard drive. This process is usually known as "ripping"; iTunes, however, calls it "Importing".

You can't really go wrong. Load a CD into your computer and it will appear in iTunes as an icon in the source list; click the icon and the CD's contents are displayed in the song list.

Get names...

If, when you originally installed iTunes, you agreed to let it connect to the Internet whenever it feels it needs to, then within a few seconds of loading the CD you'll probably find that the artist, track and album names – and maybe more info besides – automatically appear in the song list. This information is not pulled from the CD, which contains nothing but music. Rather, it's downloaded via the Internet from CDDB – a giant CD information database hosted by a company called Gracenote (www.gracenote.com).

If iTunes isn't set to connect to the Net automatically, you'll need to tell the program to try and download the track info from CDDB. Connect to the Internet and then select "Get CD Track Names" from the Advanced menu in iTunes.

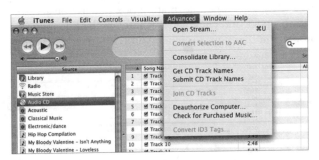

If you get no joy from CDDB resource, the songs will be left with the titles "Track 1", "Track 2" and so on, and you'll have to input the track info manually (see overleaf). This happens remarkably infrequently, but it's highly likely that the info downloaded may either be inaccurate or won't tally with your own ideas of music categorization – one person's hip-hop is another's R&B, after all. In either case, you'll need to edit the information manually.

> **TIP: If you rip a few CDs to a laptop when you're out and about and can't get online, you can always access the CDDB database later.**
> Simply select the track or tracks in question and click "Get CD Track Names" from the Advanced menu.

Adding and editing track info manually

You can enter information directly into any editable field of the song list by clicking on its name twice (not too quickly). Any existing text will become highlighted and you're ready to type. When you're done, click somewhere else in the window or hit Enter.

Alternatively, to view, add or edit all kinds of information about a track, select it in the song list and hit Apple+I (Mac) or Ctrl+I (PC). The same information box can also be accessed by selecting a track and clicking "Get Info" in the File menu or the mouse menu that pops up when you right-click (Ctrl+click on a Mac) a track.

	Song Name	Artist ▲	Time	Album	Genre
6	☑ Body And Soul	Billie Holiday	3:26	Lady In Autumn: The Bes...	Jazz
7	☐ Strange Fruit			In Autumn: The Bes...	Jazz
8	☑ (There Is) No Greater L	iTunes Help		In Autumn: The Bes...	Jazz
9	☑ Stormy Weather	Get Info		In Autumn: The Bes...	Jazz
10	☑ God Bless The Child	Show Song File		In Autumn: The Bes...	Jazz
11	☑ Do Nothin' Till You He	My Rating ▶		In Autumn: The Bes...	Jazz
12	☑ Don't Explain	Reset Play Count		In Autumn: The Bes...	Jazz
13	☑ Fine And Mellow	Convert ID3 Tags...		In Autumn: The Bes...	Jazz
14	☑ Life Begins When You'r	Convert Selection to AAC		Quintessential Billie ...	Jazz
15	☑ It's Like Reaching For			Quintessential Billie ...	Jazz
16	☑ These Foolish Things	Play Next in Party Shuffle		Quintessential Billie ...	Jazz
17	☑ I Cried For You			Quintessential Billie ...	Jazz

Multiple tracks

To edit or enter information about multiple songs simultaneously, simply select the relevant tracks in the song list (see the tip box below) and press Ctrl+I or Apple+I (or right-click and press "Get Info"). In the Multiple Song Information box that

> **TIP: To select multiple tracks in the song list, hold down the Apple key (Mac) or Ctrl key (PC) as you click. To select a range, click the first and last track while holding the Shift key.**

will pop up, as soon as you make any changes to a field, the box to its left becomes checked. Before you hit "OK", make sure only the fields you want to change are checked.

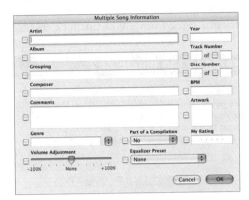

The Multiple Song Information box offers a whole lot more than just basic artist and album details. For more on Equalizer and Volume settings, see p.114.

> ▶ **TIP:** If iTunes downloads incorrect or non-existent song info and you have to do some manual entering or editing, select "Submit CD Track Names" from the iTunes Advanced menu once you're done. Then other people accessing the CDDB service will be able to benefit from your handiwork.

Track info shortcut keys

Open the track info window	**Apple+I**
Next pane in the track info window	**Apple+]**
Previous pane in the Get Info window	**Apple+[**
Show info for the next track in the song list	**Apple+N**
Show info for the previous track in the song list	**Apple+P**

Importing your tracks

OK, now you've sorted out the track details, it's time to import your CD's songs into the iTunes Library. To the left of each song title in the song list you'll see a checked tick box; if you don't wish to import a particular track from a CD, uncheck its box.

Where does the music go?

Unless you change the settings, each imported song is saved as an individual file in a hierarchy of folders which reside within your iTunes folder. This can be found within either your Music folder (Mac) or My Documents folder (PC). The hierarchy is defined by the artist and album information of each track. For example, The Beatles' "Dig A Pony" can be tracked down via the following route:

iTunes ▶ iTunes Music ▶ The Beatles ▶ Let It Be ▶ Dig A Pony

As you start to stock your iTunes Library, it becomes important to remain consistent in the way you label your music, or you could end up with multiple entries (and folders) for a single artist. Details retrieved from CDDB are invariably inconsistent (one CD may yield "The Beatles" as the artist, while another might appear labelled "Beatles, The", or simply "Beatles"). Though these kind of discrepancies don't have any detrimental effect on the way iTunes performs, they can be very annoying when you are browsing for songs on either your computer or your iPod.

Now hit the large, round "Import" button in the upper right-hand corner of the iTunes window and watch as each of your selections is copied to your hard drive.

> ▶ **TIP:** Many new iTunes users assume that playlists are the primary tools for arranging songs into albums, and create a new one for every CD they import. This a waste of time and source-list space. To view all your albums, simply use the Browse function (see p.47).

Joining tracks

Before importing the tracks from a CD, it's possible to "join" some of them together. Then, when they're played back on your computer or your iPod, they'll always stay together as one unit, and iTunes won't insert a gap between the tracks. This is useful if you have an album in which two or more tracks are segued together (the end of one song merging into the beginning of the next) or if you just think certain tracks should always be heard together (if you joined the three movements of a symphony, for example, the whole work will appear together when you're playing in shuffle mode).

To do this, simply select the tracks you want to join and then click "Join CD Tracks" from the Advanced menu. In the short term you can change your mind by clicking "Unjoin CD Tracks", but once you've pressed "Import", the songs will be imported as a single audio file that cannot be separated without the use of audio-editing software (see p.124).

▲	Song Name
1	☑ ┌ Mara
2	Timo Ma
3	Phaser
4	Danny T
5	Sandra (
6	└ Stef

Import preferences

The Importing Preferences pane, which provides various options relating to the way in which the import process works, can be found within the iTunes Preferences window, opened via the iTunes menu (Mac) or the Edit menu (PC).

The first two dropdown menus relate to the file format that iTunes uses when it copies songs into the Library; these settings are important and are covered in full in later chapters. The remaining three checkboxes are pretty self-explanatory.

When "Play songs while importing" is selected, iTunes will start to play the new album once the first song has been imported. This feature can cause the import process to be considerably slower, and if the first track of your CD is very short iTunes can get ahead of itself and try to play something that hasn't yet finished importing, which might cause the application to crash.

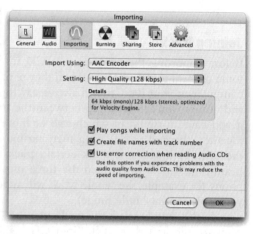

Preferences shortcut keys

	Mac	PC
Open Preferences	Apple+,	Ctrl+,
Next pane within Preferences window	Apple+]	
Previous pane within Preferences window	Apple+[	

Before closing the Preferences panel, click the General tab. Here you can choose how iTunes deals with CDs when they are inserted into your computer. From the "On CD insert" drop-down menu you can ask iTunes to automatically start the import process and also eject a CD when it's finished: this is very useful when you are ripping CD after CD, conveyor-belt style.

> ▶ **TIP: One thing to think about very early on is what file format and sound quality you want to import your music at. You don't want to have to re-rip all your CDs a few months down the line if you decide that you're not happy with the sound, or you want to use the tracks with an MP3 player that doesn't support Apple's default AAC format. For more on all of this, turn to p.103.**

Browsing and searching

Though some people manage to use iTunes for months without ever noticing it, the "Browse" option is a very important iTunes feature, allowing you to browse quickly and easily by genre, artist and album. To open Browse mode, clicking

Browse

the eye icon on the toolbar (it may be missing in some circumstances) or by selecting Show Browser from the Edit menu.

> ▶ **TIP: You'll be using the Browse mode a lot, so for quick access get used to using the relevant keyboard shortcuts: Apple+B (on a Mac) or Ctrl+B (on a PC).**

using iTunes & the iPod

Browse mode introduces a panel above the song list. This should automatically include artist and album; if you also want a genre column (which is a good idea), you can turn this option on under the General pane of iTunes Preferences. In the same pane you can choose whether you want albums that iTunes recognizes as compilations to appear in the Browse-mode "Artist" column.

Browsing is simple. Clicking an entry under "Genre" reveals the artists from that genre; clicking an entry under "Artists", in turn, reveals all the albums of that artist. And, with each selection, the song list changes to display only the relevant songs.

> **TIP: You can edit track info from the Browse lists, which is useful for quickly changing all "Beatles" tracks, say, to "The Beatles". Simply select a genre, artist or album and press Apple+I (Mac) or Ctrl+I (PC).**

Searching

The Search box, on the right-hand side at the top of the iTunes environment, lets you find a track by typing all or part of the name of the artist, album or song title (if you only

want to search one of these fields, use the dropdown menu that appears when you hit the magnifying glass icon).

Note, though, that iTunes will only search those tracks currently in the song list. So if you want to search your whole collection, make sure that the Library icon is selected in the source list, and "All" is selected in the "Genre" column before you start to type.

Deleting music

There are several ways to delete music from the iTunes Library. However you do it, first make sure that Library is selected in the source list and then select the songs you want to ditch in the song list. Deleting files from a playlist (see p.65) does not delete the actual file from the iTunes Library – only the playlist's reference to the file.

If you want to select and delete multiple tracks, hold down the Apple or Ctrl key while clicking in the songlist. Alternatively,

click on the first and then Shift+click the last; individual songs can then be removed from this selected group by clicking them while holding down the Apple key (Mac) or the Ctrl key (PC). Or, if you want to remove an artist or whole album from your collection, open the Browse mode and select the relevant entry in the list.

Then, either...

▶ Hit Backspace on your keyboard.

▶ Select Clear from the iTunes Edit menu.

▶ Ctrl+click (Mac) or right-click (PC) the items and select Clear from the mouse menu.

▶ On a Mac you can also drag the selections straight to the Trash.

> **TIP: Deleting music as described above will send the files to your Recycle Bin or Trash, ready to be permanently deleted. If you want to remove something from iTunes but not actually delete it from your computer, right-click on the song and select "Show Song File" to view the file in Finder or Windows Explorer. Copy this file somewhere else, and then return to iTunes and remove the file.**

04

iPod
quickstart

what you need to know

etting a new iPod up and running really is a piece of cake. But there are quite a few options and features – both on the iPod itself and in the way it interacts with iTunes – that may pass you by. So, while some of what follows is self-explanatory, you're sure to learn something…

The iPod – your first time

Your iPod should have come with a FireWire cable that will allow you to connect both to your computer and to the supplied power adapter (see box). Depending on which model you bought, you may also have got a USB2 cable, which you can ignore unless you are a PC user lacking a FireWire socket on your computer. If you lack a FireWire socket and your iPod wasn't supplied with a USB2 plug, you'll have to purchase one separately.

Your iPod may also have come with a Dock – a little stand designed to provide a secure spot for your iPod and to make it easy for you to connect to both a computer and a hi-fi (see p.119). Plug the flat end of the cable either into the back of the Dock or directly into the base of your iPod; and attach the other end to your computer's FireWire or USB port. The iPod's display should change to tell you not to disconnect.

The flat connector slots into your iPod or Dock. When disconnecting, be sure to press the (nearly invisible) release buttons on the sides of the connector.

Charging

Your iPod will have come with a power plug bearing a FireWire socket, which allows you to recharge the battery using the same cable that you use to connect to your computer. However, most people will find that their computer is also capable of recharging their iPod. This is true of all recent Macs and many PCs, depending on the specific model of iPod and whether the PC has a powered FireWire or USB2 socket. The most reliable way to test this (as the iPod's charging battery icon can occasionally mislead) is to allow your battery to go completely flat and then see if the computer successfully recharges it. Note, though, that even if you can recharge via your computer, it will only work when your computer is on and not in sleep/standby mode.

To completely recharge from empty typically takes a few hours and provides around eight hours of music playback. Just leaving the Pod lying around and not playing, however, will also cause the power level to gradually drain. For tips on maximizing your battery life, see p.196.

If this is the first time you've attached your iPod, you'll be invited to choose a name for it, which is no laughing matter (see box overleaf). And iTunes should launch automatically, showing an icon for your iPod in the Source list. If you later decide that you don't want iTunes to launch when you connect your Pod – because, for example, this can be annoying when you are using the device as a hard drive (see p.155) – you can disable this function in the iPod Preferences panel (see p.55).

Automatic updates

By default, your iPod will be set to automatically syncronize itself with the contents of your iTunes Library, making an exact match of all your songs and playlists (see p.63) whenever you connect. All you have to do is sit back and wait for a message in the iTunes Status area informing you that the update is complete. The first time you do this it can take a while, but after that it typically only takes a minute or two, depending on how many new songs you've added since your last update.

The name game

Judging by the number of online chat forums devoted to the subject, naming an iPod is a serious business. The obvious move is to call it "John's Pod", "Jane's Pod", or whatever, but we think you can do better than that. Here are a few weird and wonderful ideas plucked from the World Wide Web:

"I was thinking and thinking of a name for my mini ... I looked up Greek and Latin roots and named it 'Parfichlorolocuphone', which means small, green, sound speaker..."

GreenerMini

"doPi (ipod backward) the music elf, as in harry potter rip off of dobby the house elf..."

tombo_jombo

"My iPod's name is 'Glitch', because I had to set it up with Win98SE..."

jesspark

For more inspiration, search Google Groups (www.google.com/groups), or search "Does your iPod have a name" in the forums section of iPodLounge (www.ipodlounge.com/forums).

If you've already named your iPod, it's not too late to change it: just double-click its name in the iTunes Source list and type something else. But be sure to bear in mind this essential advice...

"Its not bad to change the iPod's name as long as you sit down with it and have a long conversation about what it thinks is best for it."

Kurt8374

It's worth noting that this sync will also delete tracks: if there's something on your iPod that's not on your computer, it will be removed when you perform an update. Also, it's a one-way process, reproducing your iTunes Library on your iPod – not the other way around. So you can't easily add new songs to your iPod from someone else's computer and then have them automatically move over to your computer (though there are workarounds for this; see p.182).

Manual updates

As we've already mentioned, if you don't want iTunes to jump into action every time you connect your iPod, you can easily stop this happening in the iPod Preferences panel (see below). Within this panel you'll also find options for stopping iTunes automatically updating your iPod. There are two choices.

To open the iPod Preferences panel, select the iPod icon in the Source list and then click the iPod button that appears at the bottom of iTunes.

Alternatively, Ctrl+click (Mac) or right-click (PC) the icon of your Pod in the Source list and press iPod Options.

iPod Preferences

◉ Automatically update all songs and playlists
◯ Automatically update selected playlists only:

☐ Bach/Gould
☐ Beethoven
☐ Choral
☐ Classical General
☐ Comps

◯ Manually manage songs and playlists

☐ Open iTunes when attached
☑ Enable disk use
☑ Only update checked songs

(Cancel)　(OK)

Automatically update selected playlists only

This option is useful if you want to save time when connecting; you have an iPod without the capacity to hold your whole collection; or you're using multiple iPods with a single copy of iTunes (each user can simply organize their own material within a specific set of playlists). For more on playlists, see p.63.

> **Tip:** You can only access iPod Preferences when the Pod is attached. But if your iPod is set to update automatically and you want to stop this happening, hold down Apple+Alt (Mac) or Ctrl+Alt (PC) for a few seconds while attaching the iPod.

Manually manage songs and playlists

This gives you complete control over the contents of your iPod. When selected, you update your Pod by dragging tracks, albums, playlists, genres or artists from the iTunes Library onto the iPod icon in the Source list. You can also drag directly into any playlists on the iPod (click the small triangle next to the iPod's icon in the Source list to view them).

In this "manual mode" you can also remove songs or playlists from your iPod: click the Pod's icon; select either one or more items from the song list; Ctrl+click (Mac) or right-click (PC) them; and select "Clear" from the dropdown menu. It's worth noting, however, that, as in iTunes, removing a song from a playlist only removes it from the playlist – not from the iPod.

> **Tip:** None of these various sync and manual modes allow you to copy songs from an iPod to iTunes. But this can be done (see p.182).

Disconnecting

Depending on a few factors, an attached iPod may display the warning "Do not disconnect". If so, you'll need to "unmount" your iPod before unplugging the cable. To do this, either:

 Click the eject icon to the right of the iPod icon in the Source list (see below).

 Click the eject button in the bottom-right corner of the iTunes window (see below).

 Ctrl+click (Mac) or right-click (PC) the iPod icon in the Source list and select "Eject…".

 On a Mac you can also eject your Pod by dragging its Desktop icon to the trash (only with Hard Disk Mode enabled, see p.155).

If you simply disconnect the device without properly dismounting it, you could end up mashing song data, crashing your computer or even damaging the hard drive in your iPod, so get into the habit of doing it properly. And even when following one of the correct procedures, don't physically pull the plug, or remove your Pod from the Dock, until the iPod's screen displays the regular menu. On older Pods a large tick icon appears to inform you that the dismount was successful.

If the iPod refuses to unmount, and the "Do not disconnect" message stays on the screen, there may be a problem. Turn to the Troubleshooting chapter (see p.193).

The iPod controls

Once your Pod's loaded up with tunes and disconnected from your computer, you're ready to start exploring the various buttons and menus. Again, these are very straightforward, though there are more options than at first meet the eye.

The controls

The iPod controls have altered slightly with each new design, but whichever model you have, they're pretty intuitive (though the sensitivity of touch required may lead to gritting of teeth at first). Opposite is a rundown of what each button does on the current-generation iPod; besides those mentioned, there are also button combinations used for troubleshooting and resetting (see p.195).

iPod Minis have similar controls to their larger siblings, but with the four buttons integrated at the four compass points of the scroll wheel.

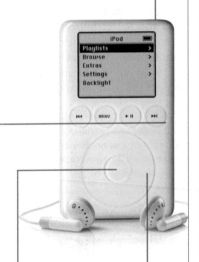

◄◄ A single click takes you back to the start of a track, a second click and you're back at the start of the previously played track (not necessarily the previous track in the album or playlist); hold down this button and you skip-search back through the currently playing track.

MENU As well as taking you back through the menus when clicked, this button turns on the iPod's backlight when held down.

▶ II The iPod doesn't have a "stop" button; instead, you simply pause and unpause the music with this button. It also turns the iPod off when held down.

▶▶I Just like the back skip/rewind button, only forwards.

Hold switch Get used to using this to disable the other controls – especially when you're not using your iPod. There are few things more annoying than running out of juice (or even blowing headphones) because of accidental clicks.

Select button Use this to make selections in menus, or start playing a highlighted song. When a tune is playing, the button also selects between volume, rating and scrubbing (see p.60). And, held down, it adds tracks to On-The-Go playlist (see p.61).

Scroll wheel Besides letting you scroll through menus, this wheel also alters the volume when you're listening to music.

Browsing the menus

The iPod's hierarchy of menus and submenus is pretty self-explanatory, and best explored by trial and error, so we won't patronize or bore you with a complete walk-through here. Suffice to say that you browse to a track, album or playlist and press the Select button to set it

going. If you find yourself lost, simply backtrack using the Menu button until you know where you are again.

Here are a few tips and tricks to ease your browsing and help you get the most from your Pod's controls...

▶ By default the iPod clicks repeatedly whenever you touch either the scroll wheel or a button. As well as being a slight waste of battery power, this will win you no friends when travelling on public transport. To disable the clicks, scroll to Settings, then Clicker, and use the Select button to choose Off.

▶ Under Main Menu in Settings, you can choose exactly which browsing categories you want to access from your Pod's top-level menu. Classical buffs, for example, will definitely want to add "Composer".

▶ If your menus are hard to read, navigate to Contrast, within Settings, and use the scroll wheel to adjust the setting.

▶ "Scrubbing" means speeding through a song visually, rather than aurally. When a track is playing, hit the Select button once and you should see a little diamond shape representing your current position in the song. Move this forwards or backwards using the scroll wheel and then press Select.

On-The-Go playlists

If you're out and about and you want to set up a playlist there and then, you can do so with the iPod's On-The-Go playlist function. Browse your library and when you come across a song you'd like to add, press and hold the Select button. After around a second the track's name will flash three times to let you know that it has been added to the On-The-Go playlist. Navigate to the next song you want to add and repeat the process. You can then access the new playlist like any other – within the Playlists menu.

▶ Pressing the Select button twice will allow you to rate a track (see p.81).

▶ When listening to one track, you can browse through the other tracks and menus as usual – just press Menu and off you go. If you do this, however, you won't be able to use the scroll wheel to either scrubb or change the volume and rating until you return to the track you are currently playing. To do this return to the main menu and then choose Currently Playing (at the bottom of the list).

▶ When browsing through tracks, holding down the Select button for a couple of seconds will add a highlighted song to the iPod's "On-The-Go" playlist (see box).

▶ To see how much space you have left on the iPod, click About within the Settings menu. This function can be unreliable, though, so if you want to be certain, attach your iPod to your computer and look on the bottom of the iTunes windows.

▶ Within the Settings menu you can turn on Repeat and Shuffle modes (see p.68). However, bear in mind that if your iPod is set to play forever, you'll be more likely to run down your battery (or damage your earphones) if you forget to use the Hold switch and the Pod gets turned on accidentally in your pocket.

using iTunes & the iPod

> ▶ **TIP: Be careful if exploring the Language settings.
> If you accidentally choose a language you don't
> understand, you may struggle to get things back to
> how they were. If this happens, see p.196 for help.**

The remote control

There's not much to say about the remote control that ships with some iPod models and is available separately for some others (see p.174). It sits between your iPod and earphones, allowing easy access to basic functions such as play, pause, volume, next/previous track and Hold. It's certainly handy if your Pod is usually buried deep in a pocket or bag, but it can also be annoying, since many of the most useful functions are inaccessible and it adds extra bulk and length to the earphone cable.

Crash!

It probably won't be long before your iPod does something strange – such as stops responding when you press the buttons. In situations such as this, you'll need to reset your Pod. See p.195 for instructions.

05
Playtime

playlists and other player functions

A key feature of any computer jukebox software is the ability to create playlists: homemade combinations of tracks for playing on your computer or iPod; for burning to CD; for sending to friends; or even for publishing online. Like the old-fashioned mix tape, a playlist can be made for a particular time, place or person, or just for fun. Unlike with cassettes, however, playlists can be created instantly; they can be as long as you like; they won't be poor sound quality; and there's no need to buy physical media. iTunes provides plenty of playlist tools as well as other modes and functions that relate to playing music. All is explained in this chapter...

Playlists

The first thing to understand about playlists is that they don't actually contain any music. All they contain is a list of pointers to tracks within your iTunes Library. This means you can delete playlists, and individual tracks within them, without deleting the actual music files; likewise, you can add the same track to as many playlists as you like without using up extra disk space.

Playlists appear in the Source list (along with the icons for Library, Radio, etc) and they're completely editable at any time. You can drag one or more songs into a playlist from the song list, or – using Browse mode – you can even drag in an entire artist, genre or album's contents in one fell swoop. Once a playlist is highlighted in the Source list, its contents become available in the song list, allowing you to play, delete or rearrange the tracks at will. And, next time you update, your playlists will be copied across to your iPod, and appear in the top-level menu.

iTunes probably came with a few Smart Playlists (more on what this means below) labelled "60's Music", "My Top Rated", etc. Don't be scared to delete them.

Creating playlists

To create a new playlist, either hit the new playlist button (the +) at the bottom of the Source list, or press Apple+N (Mac) or Ctrl+N (PC). Either way, a new playlist icon will appear in the Source list, highlighted and ready to be named and filled. Try it: create and name a playlist; click on the Library icon to view all your music; and drag some random tracks onto your playlist's icon.

You can also create a new playlist by dragging songs, artists, albums or genres directly into some blank space at the end of the Source list. A new playlist of those cuts will appear and iTunes will even try to name it according to the tracks being dragged (you can always change it manually; see below).

> ▶ **TIP: You'll find a "New playlist from selection"**
> **option in the Edit menu. Holding Shift and**
> **clicking the new playlist button (Mac) or**
> **pressing Ctrl+Shift+N (PC) has the same effect.**

Rearranging, renaming and deleting playlists

You can sort the contents of a playlist automatically by clicking the top of the columns in the song list. Or, to sort them manually, first sort by the number column and then drag the tracks at will.

To rename a playlist, click its name once and then again (not too fast). To delete one, highlight it and press the backspace key; select Clear from the Edit or right-click meus; or, on a Mac, drag the icon into the Trash.

> ▶ **TIP: If you want to delete a playlist without**
> **being asked to confirm, hold down Apple**
> **(Mac) or Ctrl (PC) while you hit backspace. Or,**
> **to make this the default option, check "Do not ask**
> **me again" in the confirmation box.**

Smart Playlists

Smart Playlists are just like normal playlists but, rather than being compiled manually by you, iTunes does the work on your behalf, collecting all tracks in your Library that fulfil a set of rules, or

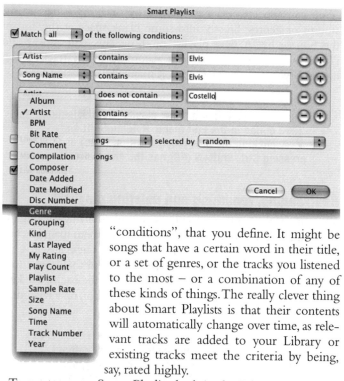

"conditions", that you define. It might be songs that have a certain word in their title, or a set of genres, or the tracks you listened to the most – or a combination of any of these kinds of things. The really clever thing about Smart Playlists is that their contents will automatically change over time, as relevant tracks are added to your Library or existing tracks meet the criteria by being, say, rated highly.

To create a new Smart Playlist, look in the Edit menu or click the New Playlist button while holding down Alt (Mac) or Shift (PC) – you'll see the plus sign change into a cog. This will open the Smart Playlist box (as shown above), where you set the parameters for the new list. Simply click **+** and **−** to add and remove rules. It's a bit like a bizarre kind of musical algebra.

To edit the rules of an existing Smart Playlist, select it and choose "Edit Smart Playlist" in the File menu – or in the menu you get by right-clicking (PC) or Ctrl-clicking (Mac).

Smart Playlist ideas

Smart Playlists give you the opportunity to be creative with the way you organize the songs in your Library; they can be both a lot of fun and very useful. So much so, in fact, that there are whole websites devoted to the subject (see www.smartplaylists.com).

Following are a few examples to give you an idea of the kind of things you can do with Smart Playlist.

Functional...

Tracks I've never heard
▶ Play Count is 0
Lets you hear music that you've ripped or downloaded but not yet played.

On the up
▶ Date Added is in the last 30 days
▶ My Rating is greater than 3 stars
▶ Play Count is less than 5
A playlist of new songs that you like, but which deserve more of a listen.

The old Johanna
▶ Grouping contains piano
If you use Grouping or Comment fields (see p.81) to tag tracks by instrument, mood or anything else, you can then create Smart Playlists based on this info.

And inspirational...

A compilation of questions
▶ Song Name contains "?"
For days with no answers.

Space songs
▶ Song Name contains "space"
▶ Song Name contains "stars"
▶ Song Name contains "moon"
▶ Song Name contains "rocket"
For those who love their sci-fi as much as their music.

Play modes

In its default state, iTunes will play whatever is in the song list, in the order shown in the song list, and then stop. But there are various other options…

> **TIP: On the iPod, you can choose between the various Shuffle and Repeat modes within the Settings menu. But you won't find Party Shuffle.**

Repeat

Most CD players offer you the option of playing a single track or album on "loop" – round and round until you beg it to stop. And so it is with iTunes: select "Repeat All" and whatever is in the song list (whether it's an album, a playlist, a CD or your whole Library) will play round and round forever. Select "Repeat One" and only the track currently playing will loop. You can access these options via the Controls menu or with the repeat button underneath the Source list.

Shuffle

When the Shuffle option is turned on, iTunes plays back whatever is on the song list in random order – though random isn't quite the right word (see box below). This function can be toggled on and off by using either the Controls menu or the Shuffle button below the Source list.

> ▶ TIP: If you have Shuffle mode on and you want to see what's coming next, simply click the top of the track number column in the song list. If you don't like the order iTunes has selected, reshuffle by turning Shuffle mode off and back on, or by holding hold down Alt (Mac) or Shift (PC) and clicking the Shuffle button once.

How random is Shuffle?

Though there's no such thing as true random-order generation, computers and their programmers can do an excellent job of simulating genuine disorder. But many iTunes and iPod users have complained of a distinct presence of pattern, even predictability, in the "random" selections generated by the Shuffle mode. Perhaps it's just superstition – no one outside Apple HQ seems to know how Shuffle actually works – but people claim to hear certain artists or tunes appearing more than others, and genres or artists appearing in chunks rather than evenly spread out.

If you read about the subject online, you'll find all sorts of theories as well as many supposed solutions. You could try, for example, sorting your tracks by track name (though two versions of the same tune will appear together, as will all "Sonatas", for example). Or, if you want to ensure that you never hear one track until you've heard all the rest, create a Smart Playlist for songs which have a Play Count of less than 2 (though once you've gone all the way, you'll have to change the Play Count setting to 3).

Party Shuffle

Party Shuffle, found in the Source list, is a play mode that generates a random mix of tracks drawn from either a playlist of your choice or your entire Library. When Party Shuffle is being used, a new panel appears at the bottom of the song list, in which you can set parameters for how the list looks and where the tracks are drawn from, though you can also add selections from anywhere in your Library by dragging them onto the Party Shuffle icon in the Source list. At any time you can regenerate the tracklist either manually – by dragging them up and down – or automatically, by hitting the Refresh button in the top right corner of the iTunes Window (this will replace the list's contents with fresh selections, but not remove manually added songs).

If you don't want to see the Party Shuffle icon in the Source list, you can choose to hide it by unchecking the box under the General settings in iTunes Preferences.

Visualizer

If you are not content just to sit and watch a small dot plodding its way across the iTunes status area as your songs play, then turn on the iTunes Visualizer: a psychedelic light show that swirls and morphs in time with the music. Depending on your taste, it will either hypnotize you into a state of blissful paralysis or annoy the hell out of you.

The Visualizer can be turned on or off by clicking its button in the bottom right corner of the iTunes window (the one with the little flower-like icon). There's also a Visualizer menu where you can set how large you want the visuals to appear in the iTunes window and also turn on the full-screen mode, with which the swirling patterns take over your whole monitor, just like a screen saver.

When the Visualizer is doing its thing, the button in the top right corner of the iTunes window can be used to open the

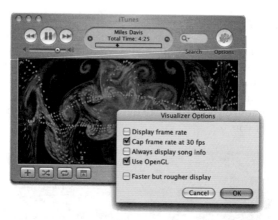

Options pane. Some of the choices are self-explanatory, but others are less so. Unchecking the "Cap frame-rate" box may allow you to improve the visuals, but will add an extra burden onto your system resources (which might, for example, slow down other applications). And "Use OpenGL" should be left checked unless you have reason to turn it off (see box below).

You can also use a number of keyboard shortcuts to adjust the settings while the Visualizer is playing.

OpenGL

OpenGL is a global standard for 3D (and 2D) computer graphics development. The idea is that with this standard in place both hardware and software developers can be sure that new machines will support applications that rely on advanced graphics, and new software that features advanced graphics will run smoothly on any machine with any operating system. However, you may find that some Visualizer plug-ins (see p.74) don't work with your iTunes setup – if this is the case, try disabling OpenGL in the Options pane. For more see:

OpenGL.org www.opengl.org

Visualizer shortcuts

▶ **Z & X** Varies the current colour scheme.

▶ **A & S** Cycles through the waveforms of the current pattern.

▶ **Q & W** Cycles through the various patterns.

▶ **R** Randomly selects a new style and colour.

▶ **C** Displays information about the current pattern (they all have fitting names, such as "diamond tiled tunnel").

▶ **M** Toggles between play modes. In "Random slideshow" mode, iTunes picks the patterns arbitrarily; in "User config slideshow", iTunes picks from your presets (see the Tip box below); in "Freezing current" mode, a single pattern continues indefinitely.

▶ **I** Displays info and cover art for currently playing track.

▶ **D** Return to default settings.

▶ **B** Places the Apple logo in the centre of the Visualizer screen (just in case you forget who you have to thank for all the patterns).

▶ **F** Displays the frame rate.

▶ **T** Turns frame-rate cap on/off.

▶ **?** Displays a list of shortcut keys on-screen.

> ▶ **TIP:** If you see a pattern you like, hold down Shift and a number key (0–9). Then you can recall the pattern at any time by pressing the relevant key. And if you turn on "User config slideshow" with the M key, iTunes will combine your preset choices.

Visualizer plug-ins

If you get bored of the built-in iTunes visuals you can always add more. There are loads to be found online, at sites such as:

Arkaos www.arkaos.net
JCode www.jcode.org
PluginsWorld.com www.pluginsworld.com

Once you've downloaded some plug-ins, they're very easy to install. On a Mac, drag them to the iTunes Plug-ins folder (which can be found within iTunes, within Library, within your Home folder); or, if you have multiple users set up on your computer and you want the plug-in to be available to all, drag them to the iTunes Plug-ins folder located in the iTunes folder in the main Library folder of your Macintosh HD (if the iTunes Plug-ins folder isn't there, create it). On a PC, the iTunes Plug-ins folder can be found in the iTunes folder within the My Music folder. Again, if there isn't one there, create a new folder.

Start/stop times

If you've long been bugged by something at the beginning or end of a track – an extended fade, a concert recording applause, a snippet of indulgent band banter, or whatever – now is your change to excise it. Whether you've ripped the track from CD or downloaded it, it can be topped and tailed in iTunes.

Let's take, for example, The Beatles' "Good Morning, Good Morning", which opens with the crow of a cockerel. If you listened to the song and kept an eye on the iTunes status area,

> **TIP:** If you want songs in iTunes to melt into each other seamlessly, open Preferences and, under Audio, mess around with the "Crossfade playback" settings.

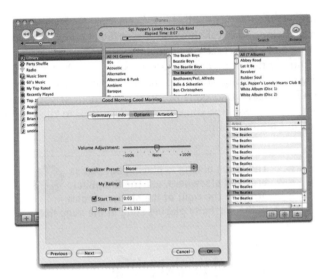

you'd see that the cockerel's moment of glory lasts a good two seconds, and the band don't start playing until the display reads "Elapsed time: 0.03".

To erase the offending bird, we first need to select the track in the song list and select "Get Info" from the File menu. Under the Options panel in the box that pops up, there are boxes for the song's current Start Time (which, as you might expect, is 0:00) and Stop Time. Now we can simply highlight the start time and type a new value – in this example, 0:03 seconds. Then we can click OK and listen back to the song to see if the new

> **TIP: For more serious editing of tracks – from trimming them to combining them – you'll need to use a wave-editing program. See p.124.**

setting is accurate enough. If not, we can go back into the Options pane and tweak the time – entering fractions of a second after a colon, if necessary (eg 0:03:50).

Trimming the end works in just the same way. And whichever end you're changing, you're not harming the song file, only the way iTunes plays it, so none of this is permanent. If you felt bad about the cockerel, say, you could simply return to the Options panel and reinstate him.

> **TIP: When a song is playing but you've browsed elsewhere, use the SnapBack arrow in the right of the status window to show the currently playing song in the song list.**

Minimizing and miniaturizing

As with any other program, iTunes windows can be resized by dragging the bottom right corner, and also minimized – hidden from view but still active and accessible via the Dock (on a Mac) or Taskbar (in PC). This is done in the normal way: on a Mac, click the small yellow button in the top left corner of the window, or press Apple+M; on a PC, click the minimize button on the window's top right corner, or press M while holding down the Windows key.

This is all standard stuff, but, unlike most other programs, iTunes also provides a halfway house between a window being open and minimized: a miniaturized unit that offers access to the essential player control and, if desired, the status display.

This is great if you want to keep an eye on what's playing, skip tracks you don't like, and so on, while working in another program. To transform iTunes into a miniaturized player, click the small green button in the top left of the window (Mac) or press Ctrl+M (PC). The mini player that pops up can be further shunk by dragging its corner.

> **TIP:** On a Mac you can also access a menu of the most useful iTunes controls by clicking and holding the mouse over the iTunes icon on the OS X Dock. The PC version offers something similar via the iTunes icon in the System Tray (by the clock).

Problems playing songs

There are several reasons why a song might not play, but in most cases iTunes will inform you what the problem is. If it fails to offer an explanation, however, check the following:

▶ **Is the volume turned up?** Check that both the iTunes volume slider and your computer's master volume are turned up.

▶ **Are you authorized?** If you have exceeded the number of machines on which you are allowed to play your purchased tunes (see p.134) then they won't play until you deauthorize another machine and authorize the one you are trying to use. Equally, if you are trying to stream shared music (see p.96) from someone elses machine and you have not been authorized to hear their selections you will have no luck.

▶ **Is it an iTunes AAC file?** Though a track that you've found online may appear to be an AAC file (see p.104), if it wasn't created in iTunes or purchased from the iTunes Music Store (see p.129) you may not be able to play it.

▶ **Is your Internet connection too slow?** If you are having problems playing streaming previews from the iTunes Music Store, you might find it better to download the entire preview before hearing it. Open iTunes Preferences, and under Store and check the "Load complete preview before playing" box.

▶ **Does your playlist contain previews?** Playlists that contain previews (see p.133) copied from the iTunes Music Store will halt the playback of a playlist after each preview; you'll need to double-click the next song in the playlist to hear it.

> **TIP: If a song is very quiet – perhaps an old recording, say – select it, click "Get Info" in the File menu, and under Options boost its level using the Volume Adjustment slider. You can also do this for multiple songs at once.**

06
Managing your music

iTunes housekeeping

s we saw in Chapter 3 (see p.33), each song in iTunes is "tagged" with an artist name, track name and album name – information which you can either enter manually or pull off the Gracenote CD database via the Net. But, besides these three basic tagging categories, there are around twenty others, ranging from composer to sample rate – and the more info you add, the more flexibility you'll have to sort you music or create Smart Playlists. This chapter takes a brief look at tagging and managing your music – including adding cover art.

Tagging

Select a few tracks at random and the choose "Get Info" from the File menu or right-click menu. When the Multiple Song Information box appears, explore the various fields available for data. Many of them may already be filled with info downloaded from the CDDB (see p.41), but some will probably be empty and deserve a little more explanation. These are the categories that really come into their own when used in conjunction with Smart Playlists (see p.65). Here's a brief look at a few of the less obvious members of the tagging family:

▶ **Comment** Use this to add whatever additional info you want about the song: the personnel playing on it, the producer, the instruments used, even lyrics if you've got the time and inclination. Then you can construct some rather special Smart Playlists based on all this info.

▶ **Disc Number** When importing double albums, box sets, etc, use this field to describe which disc from the set a particular song is from, eg "1 of 3" or "2 of 4". By default iTunes inserts "1 of 1" in this column's fields.

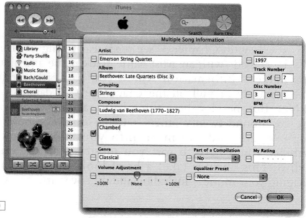

> ▶ **TIP:** You can add a rating to a track using your iPod when you are out and about. Tap the Select button twice whilst playing a song and use the scroll wheel to add a star rating. The little stars you add will find their way back into iTunes next time you sync.

▶ **My Rating** This is where you get to play music reviewer and enter a 0–5 star rating of each song – great if you want to create a Smart Playlist of your favourite tracks.

▶ **Equalizer** Lets you assign EQ presets to specific songs (see p.114).

▶ **Grouping** Like Comment, this is a useful wild-card category where you can create your own criteria for grouping and sorting songs. World music fans, for example, might enter a song's country of origin here; classical music fans might differentiate between century or instrument. Again, it's useful for both browsing and creating Smart Playlists.

▶ **BPM** Lets you specify the beats per minute of a track, which can be used to create DJ-style mixes. You could either mix tracks manually in a playlist, or sort a playlist by BPM and let iTunes do the mix with its "Crossfade" feature (see p.74). If you're into making your own music, this tag may also come in handy for picking songs of the right speed to sample.

> ▶ **TIP:** Feel free to create your own genres, rather than sticking with those in the list. If you mainly listen to jazz, say, you might want to use "bebop", "modal" and so on. Unlike when you use the Grouping field, your new genres will be easily accessible via Browse mode (see p.47).

View options

As we've seen, one good reason for adding extra info to your tracks is to create Smart Playlists. But having extra tags also allows you extra options for viewing and sorting songs in the iTunes song list.

By default, the song list doesn't contain columns for most of the various information categories. But you can add and remove columns at any time using the View Options box, which can summoned from the Edit menu or with the shortcut Apple+J (Mac) or Ctrl+J (PC). Alternatively, try Ctrl+clicking (Mac) or right-clicking (PC) the header of any of the columns in the song list to reveal a dropdown menu of columns (as shown opposite).

Once you've checked all the columns you want to see, and unchecked those you don't, your song list should change to reflect this. But that's not all. You can then rearrange the columns – by dragging their headers – into any order you want.

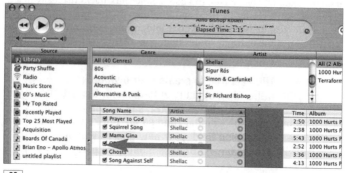

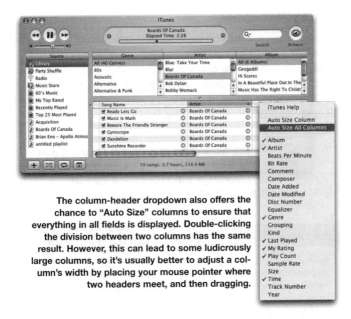

The column-header dropdown also offers the chance to "Auto Size" columns to ensure that everything in all fields is displayed. Double-clicking the division between two columns has the same result. However, this can lead to some ludicrously large columns, so it's usually better to adjust a column's width by placing your mouse pointer where two headers meet, and then dragging.

It's worth noting that these view options are not universal, but apply only to which ever item is currently highlighted in the Source list. This is very useful, since different playlists require different fields. For a dance selection, as mentioned above, you might want to view the Beats Per Minute column, while a classical playlist would obviously need the Composer column.

Besides the track info already discussed, there are a couple of extra column options which aren't user-editable:

▶ **Play Count** The number of times a song has been played in iTunes: useful for creating Smart Playlists (such as the pre-existing iTunes "Top 25 Most Played" list).

▶ **Kind** The file format of a track (see p.103).

Sorting your songs

Once you have a column in view, you can sort by it by clicking its header. Click a second time and the order is reversed (with the small black triangle on the header flipping to indicate the direction of the ordering). You can jump to a particular point in the list by pressing a letter or number: if you sort by artist and press "R", say, you might jump to The Rolling Stones.

> **TIP: The track order of a playlist is copied over to your iPod when you update. On the Pod you can't rearrange tracks, so make sure the playlists are sorted to your taste before updating.**

Multiple windows

When managing and arranging your music, don't feel obliged to keep everything confined to a single iTunes panel: double-clicking a highlighted item in the Source list will open its contents in a new floating frame.

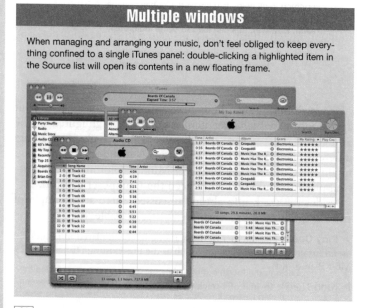

> **TIP: Either by sorting your Library or using the Browse mode (see p.47), check now and again for artists and genres listed under two different names – "N Cave", "Nick Cave", "Nick Cave & The Bad Seeds", for example. Correcting these kind of discrepancies will help to keep your iTunes folders tidy and your Smart Playlists effective.**

Adding images

iTunes lets you add "artwork" to each track. Then, when the track is playing or selected, it will show in the iTunes artwork panel (shown below). Most people who bother to take advantage of this feature go for the front cover of the album or single in question, which can usually be looted from the Internet. But,

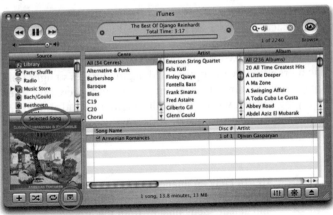

Clicking the fourth button below the Source list reveals/hides the artwork panel; clicking the title bar of the panel toggles between showing artwork for the Selected Song and Now Playing song.

using iTunes & the iPod

if you'd rather, you could choose any old picture you've found or generated. Even if you've never added any artwork, you'll probably find that you have some in your Library if you've downloaded any tracks from the iTunes Music Store (see p.129).

There are various ways to add images to a song. If you already have the image on your computer, you can drag the file directly into the artwork panel in the iTunes window, or select a track, press Apple+I (Mac) or Ctrl+I (PC), then choose Add... with the Artwork tab, and browse for the file. Alternatively, select

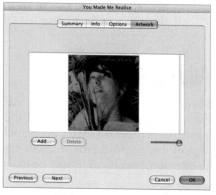

multiple tracks, artists or even genres, and use the same shortcut keys to open the Multiple Song Information box; then double-click the white Artwork box and locate the pic.

Mac users also have the option of dragging images straight from webpages or picture-viewing programs, and there are even iTunes plug-ins that wil automatically attempt to find and download the album covers to match your songs (see p.186).

> **TIP: To copy an image from a webpage, Ctrl+click (Mac) or right-click (PC) the image and select "Copy image" from the dropdown menu. The same click in the iTunes Artwork window reveals a dropdown menu with a "Paste" option.**

07

Burning CDs & DVDs

crafting compilations

As we've already seen, the playlist is the new mix tape. If you have an iPod, or your computer is hooked up to your hi-fi (see p.119), then there's little need to put your carefully compiled lists on an external medium for your own use. However, if you want to give your compilation to a friend, you'll need to burn it onto CD (or, possibly, give them the original music files; see p.98). And burning CDs and DVDs can also be a great way to back up your music. With a suitable CD or DVD drive and a copy of iTunes, none of this is very difficult.

Choices, choices

using iTunes & the iPod

If you have a CD burner on your computer, it will usually allow you to burn two types of disc: CDR (which you can write to only once) and CDRW (which can be written to many times). You can burn to these discs in various different ways, creating:

▶ **Regular audio CDs** for playing back on standard hi-fis. These can hold around 74–80 minutes of music, depending on the disc. Use CDR, not CDRW, for burning normal music discs, as they're less likely to refuse to play back on home stereos.

▶ **MP3 CDs** can store around 10–12 hours of music, but they can only include tracks in MP3 format (see p.104) and can only be played back on computers or special MP3 CD players. Again, use CDR, not CDRW, discs.

> **TIP:** If you're using iTunes with the default settings, much of your music will be in AAC format (see p.104). If you want to burn these tracks to an MP3 CD, you'll first have to convert them to MP3. See p.109 to find out how.

▶ **Data CDs** hold music as standard computer files, so can only be read by computers and a handful of clever stereos. On the plus side, they let you store about 650–750 MB of music (around 10–12 hours, depending on the sound quality) in any file format, so are useful for moving large amounts of music between computers. Both CDR and CDRW discs are good for the job.

If your computer has a DVD burner that's compatible with iTunes (and, in the case of Macs, a recent version of OS X), you can also create:

▶ **Data DVDs** These work just like data CDs, except that they can hold much more data (in most cases around 4.5 GB) and can only be read by computers with DVD drives. Useful for backing up, these can be created on either DVDR or DVDRW discs.

To choose from these various options, open the Burning tab of iTunes Preferences (see p.89). Here you can also specify a pre- ferred burning speed: leave it set to Maximum Possible unless your machine is struggling to burn a disc successfully.

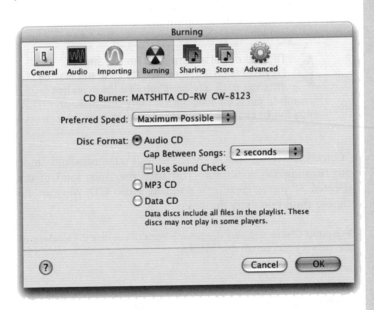

Get burning

To burn a disc in iTunes – even a data CD – you first need to arrange the relevant tracks into a playlist, as described on p.64. As you drag songs into the new list, keep an eye on the statistics at the bottom of the song list, which will tell you the total running time and file size of the selections added so far.

Depending on the specific discs that you're going to burn, you'll need to limit yourself to around 74–80 minutes for a standard audio CD, or 650 or 700 megabytes for a data or MP3 CD. The discs or their packaging should state the capacity.

If you can't resist adding more tracks than will fit on a disc, don't fret: iTunes will just burn what it can and then prompt you to insert a second disc to accommodate what's left over.

> **TIP: You can also burn a CD from a Smart Playlist (see p.65). However, its contents may be different each day, so if you like the selection enough to put it on disc, burn it there and then, or copy the tracks into a regular playlist to burn later.**

Once everything's ready, enter iTunes Preferences and, under the Burning tab, make sure you have the right kind of disc selected. If you're creating a standard audio CD, you can also choose from two extra options:

▶ **Sound Check** will alter the volume levels to equalize the loudness of the various tracks on the disc (see box).

▶ **Gaps between songs** doesn't require much explanation, though it's worth noting that these extra seconds aren't included in iTunes' estimation of the length of your playlist.

Sound Check and other options

The Sound Check function has a stab at equalizing the volume levels between tracks so that when you play back your new CD one song won't be ear-splittingly loud compared to another. This function works fine for most differences in sound level, but if you find that the songs you've combined are still irritatingly disparate on playback, try adjusting the volumes of individual tracks using the iTunes "Volume Adjustment" function (see p.112).

If that doesn't do the trick then perhaps you need to return to the source (was one song ripped from a CD and another imported from an analogue medium?) and try and figure out why a particular song has such a low noise level. Alternatively, use some audio-editing software (see p.124) to boost the volume of the quiet files.

When you're ready to create your CD, select the playlist you want to burn from the Source list and then click the "Burn Disc" button in the top-right corner of the iTunes window. It's little doors will rather pleasingly slide open to reveal a glowing black and yellow button and the iTunes status window will prompt you to insert a blank disc (you can insert a disc before this point, but you might find that iTunes promptly spits it out again).

You can also reach this point by selecting Burn Playlist to Disc from the File menu, or by right-clicking the playlist (Ctrl+click on a Mac) and choosing the option from the menu that pops up. Next, iTunes checks the disc and, when it's happy asks you, via

> ▶ **TIP:** If you want iTunes to automatically eject CDs
> when they are finished, open the General tab of
> iTunes Preferences (see p.47) and choose "Import
> songs and eject" from the "On CD Insert" menu.
> However, this will also mean that CDs will automatically
> be ripped when inserted into your computer (see p.47).

the status window, to once again hit the Burn Disc button. The burning process will take a few minutes, depending upon the speed of your hardware and the size of the playlist. When iTunes has finished its work it gives a little whistle, and within a few seconds your masterpiece appears in the iTunes Source list ready to be played or ejected.

Making covers

Half the joy of assembling a compilation has always been the painstaking delight of making the cover. These days, computers get to have all the fun; and with even a half-decent printer they can create some pretty professional-looking results.

To create a cover in iTunes, select the playlist that you've just burned – or choose a genre, artist or album in Browse mode – and select "Print" from the File menu. Alternatively, hit the keyboard shortcut Apple+P (Mac) or Ctrl+P (PC). A box will pop up offering you various options for printing the details of the playlist's contents as either a regular document or an insert for a CD jewel case – each with a number of options relating to the layout of track names and any available artwork.

When you are happy with how the cover or sheet looks (you can get a full-sized view by clicking Print and then Preview), choose Page Setup to assign printer-specific options and then hit Print.

This is all very handy, but also artistically limiting. Another option is to export your playlist's track names as a text document (see box below), and then paste them into another program that will allow you more creativity over the cover. Whichever program you intend to use – be it Microsoft Word or something more graphically serious, such as Adobe PhotoShop – you should be able to find various CD templates ready to download and fill in online. Typing the words "CD", "templates" and the name of your program into a search engine such as Google (www.google.com) should lead you to them.

> **TIP:** An alternative way to get your playlist's track details out of iTunes is to select the list's icon and then choose "Export Playlist..." from the File and right-click menus. A box appears where you can choose to save the file as a text document or an XML document. For more options, download iTunes Publisher (www.trancesoftware.com), which exports in everything from Winamp to HTML formats.

Burning problems

If you're having problems burning a CD or DVD using iTunes, check the following:

▶ **Is your drive supported?** Many CD and DVD drives that didn't come built in to an Apple computer are, currently, non-compatible with iTunes. Still, if your drive is correctly listed under Burning in iTunes Preferences, it should theoretically be fine.

▶ **Are the songs you are trying to burn protected?** Songs purchased from the iTunes Music Store are only burnable a certain number of times – perhaps the tracks you are trying to burn have already exceeded their burn privileges. If this is the case, find the CD that already features the songs (assuming you didn't post it to some distant relative) and re-import the tracks in an unprotected format.

▶ **Are you burning the right type of files?** If burning an MP3 CD, you can only include songs in the MP3 format. Turning on the "Kind" column in the song list lets you see which tracks are in which format. Also see the tip box on p.88.

▶ **Have the songs in your playlist been authorized?** If songs purchased from the iTunes Music Store have not been authorized to play on your computer, CD burning will not work. Double-click the songs in the song list and enter the ID and password for the account with which the songs was purchased. You may additionally need to deauthorize another computer if you have exceeded the maximum number of computers authorized to play the tracks (see p.134).

▶ **Does your computer go to sleep while you burn?** To stop this from happening in OS X, open System Preferences and within the Energy Saver pane increase the time before your computer sleeps. On a PC this is done in the Control Panel under Power Management.

▶ **Are you trying to play the wrong type of CD?** If you have successfully created a CD but it won't work on one or more hi-fis, double-check that you are burning a regular audio CD (see p.88) onto a CDR disc (not CDRW). Still, even if you did everything right, some CD players (especially older ones) will refuse all computer-generated CDs.

08

Sharing music

a little give and take

I n the world of digitized music, the term "sharing" is slightly ambiguous. It can refer to uncontroversial software features such as the "sharing" functions of iTunes, which allow you to listen to music stored on other computers on your home or office network. It can also refer to highly controversial practices, such as exchanging vast swathes of music with friends – the kind of thing that prompts the music industry to claim that there's no distinction between sharing copyrighted music and stealing it. This chapter looks at both these areas; for information about Internet-based peer-2-peer file sharing, see p.143.

iTunes sharing over a network

A network is two or more computers connected together, either with cables or a wireless technology such as Wi-Fi ("Airport" in Mac-speak). If you have more than one computer in the house, networking them together allows you to share files, printers and an Internet connection. If each computer is equipped with iTunes, a network also lets you "stream" music from one to another, with each computer having access to the music stored on the others – even between Macs and PCs. These days, setting up a home network can take seconds rather than days; for more info, see *The Rough Guide to the Internet* or *The Rough Guide to PCs & Windows*.

> **TIP: Sharing music over a network with iTunes has certain limitations: you can't copy or burn music from other computers, nor add it to your iPod. And the computers have to be switched on to be accessible. If you'd rather permanently copy music files from machine to machine, see p.98.**

Start sharing

First of all you'll need to set the sharing options for each computer on the network. Open iTunes Preferences (see p.46) and, under the Sharing tab, you'll see two main checkboxes: "Look for shared music" (which instructs iTunes to find shared music on other computers on the network)

and "Share my music" – which breaks down further into sharing your entire Library or just selected specified playlists. As for the "Shared name" box, whatever you enter here will pop up in the Source list of other users on the network.

Next, decide if you want to set a password for others accessing your songs: this option is not compulsory, but it could be useful if you have an open wireless network and you don't want any old passer-by tapping into your personal music collection. When you are done, click OK and start sharing.

> **TIP: Songs purchased from the iTunes Music Store can only be shared on authorized machines (see p.134).**

Listening to shared music

Once you've set up two computers to share, their icons should appear in each other's Source list. Click the icon, entering the sharer's password if required, and you can browse these selections

either directly from the song list or by clicking the small triangle to the left of the shared music icon to reveal any playlists on the shared computer. Double-click a song and then sit back and listen as the streaming starts.

> **TIP: To check whether the songs you are browsing are your own or shared, use the "Kind" column of the song list (see p.38). Shared files will appear with the word "remote" in brackets after the format type.**

Disconnecting

When you've finished with someone else's Library you "eject" it in the same way that you do a CD or your iPod: either hit the icon to the right of the shared music icon in the Source list, or hit the eject button in the bottom right of the iTunes window.

Copying music – computer to computer

The other way to share your music between computers is to literally move the music files from one to the other. It probably goes without saying that ripping a massive library of tracks from copyrighted CDs and then donating it to all your friends is against the law. But there are legitimate reasons for copying music from one computer to another: you might have two computers in the same house, say, or be upgrading to a new machine. You might also be copying music you've downloaded from the iTunes Music Store, in which case you're allowed to authorize a certain number of other computers to play each track.

First of all, you need to locate the music you want to copy, selecting either your whole iTunes folder (see p.44), or certain artist folders within it.

Then you need to move those folder to the other computer. This can be done in various ways...

▶ **Over a network** If the computers in question are already on the same network, you can enable file sharing and simply copy the artist folders you want directly from one machine to another. File sharing may already be on: if not, on a Mac, open System Preferences and look under Sharing; on a PC, right-click the iTunes folder and select Sharing and Security. For more details, search Windows or Mac OS X help.

▶ **With iPod copy software** As described on p.182, there is software available – not supported by Apple – that will allow you to pull music directly from your iPod onto any computer running iTunes.

▶ **Via an external hard drive** If you have an external hard drive (see p.190), you can back up your iTunes music folder to it and then copy the files across to the other computer. If you don't have an external drive but you do have an iPod, you could enable the iPod as a hard disk (see p.155) and use it to copy across the files.

▶ **On a CD or DVD** As explained in the previous chapter, when you burn a "data CD" (as opposed to a regular audio CD), you can fit around ten hours of music on it. A DVD can hold more like sixty hours.

> **TIP: Copying files over a network and via a CD/DVD should work fine between a PC and a Mac. However, the hard drive option will only work if the drive or iPod was formatted on a PC (see p.156).**

Importing the files

If you copied files across a network or via a hard drive (or, for that matter, downloaded them), you'll need to import them into iTunes once you have them on the target computer. This can be done by dragging the folders and/or files straight into the iTunes window or onto a specific playlist icon, or by choosing "Add Tracks to Library" from the File menu.

SERIOUS
ABOUT
SOUND

09
Music file formats
balancing sound quality and disk space

As we've already seen, importing from CD is a cinch. However, if you care about the sound quality or transferability of your music archive, you'll want to investigate the various import options. These allow you to weigh up the size of the imported music files against the fidelity of the sound and the degree to which they'll be compatible with software and hardware other than iTunes and the iPod. This chapter focuses on importing from CD, but the advice applies equally to files you've downloaded or created yourself.

serious about sound

Import options

To access the iTunes Importing options, open Preferences (from the iTunes menu on a Mac; from the Edit menu on a PC) and click on the Importing tab at the top. The two most important options are those in the dropdowns. They allow you to choose which file

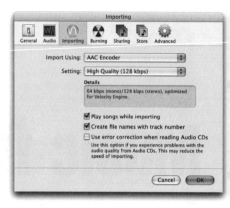

format/compression type to use, and the bitrate. If you're not sure what a file format or bitrate is, read on.

> **TIP: One problem with bigger, higher-quality music files is that, when played on an iPod, they use more battery power each second.**

Which format?

iTunes currently offers five file-format import options: AAC, MP3, AIFF, Apple Lossless and WAV. If any of these don't appear in your list of options, you're probably running an old version of iTunes. Download and install the latest version (see p.36).

The box opposite explains the pros, cons and uses of each format. But, in brief, ACC is best for day-to-day iPod and computer use; MP3 is slightly worse at the same bitrate, but can be played on any digital music player or computer (and burned onto MP3 CDs); Apple Lossless is for fidelity fanatics; and AIFF and WAV are only really for importing tracks with the aim of burning CDs.

MP3, AAC and import options

MP3 [Moving Pictures Experts Group-1/2 Audio Layer 3]
MP3 is the most common format for storing music on computer and digital music players – by quite a long way. That gives it one great advantage: if you import your music as MP3s, you can be safe in the knowledge that it will be transferable to any other player or software that you might use in the future, or which friends and family may already own. However, it no longer provides the quite best sound-quality/disk-space balance.
File name ends: .mp3
Best for: importing music you want to be able to share with non-iPod people and players, and for burning CDs to play on special MP3 CD players.

AAC [Advanced Audio Coding]
This is a relatively new encoding format, which is being pushed by Apple for two reasons. First, according to the general consensus, AAC sounds notice-ably better than MP3 when recorded at the same bitrate. Second, AAC allows Apple to embed their own DRM technology (see p.131) into files downloaded from the iTunes Music Store, to stop people freely distributing the files (MP3 DRM is a very recent phenomenon.
File name ends: .m4a (standard), .m4p (when DRM is included)
Use it for: importing music you don't expect to share with non-iPod people and players.

Apple Lossless Encoder
A recent Apple innovation, this format offers full CD quality, but only con-sumes around half the disk space – expect to fit between three and five albums per gigabyte. Currently the format only works on iTunes and iPods.
File name ends: .ale
Use it for: importing music at the highest quality for computer or iPod use.

AIFF [Advanced Interchange File Format], **WAV** [Wave]
These uncompressed formats offer the same quality as the newer Apple Lossless Encoder but they take up twice as much disk space. In their favour, however, they can be played back on nearly any computer software and also imported into audio-editing programs. Also, you might find that CDs import slightly more quickly than with Apple Lossless.
File name ends: .aiff, .wav
Use it for: importing music for burning onto CD and then deleting, or for edit-ing with audio software, but not for general playback use on iTunes or an iPod.

Note that all file formats can be burned to audio CDs and played back in normal hi-fis – it's only when sharing actual music files with non-iTunes or non-iPod equipment that compatibility becomes an issue.

> **TIP:** It's fine to mix different file formats and bitrates in your Library. Indeed, this is a sensible plan as some kinds of music will receive little benefit from high-bitrate encoding. Very sludgy, stoner-type rock, for example, may not require the same fidelity as a carefully regulated Fazioli grand piano.

Which bitrate?

As already explained (see p.19), the bitrate is the amount of data that each second of sound is reduced to. The higher the bitrate, the higher the sound quality, but also the more disk space the track takes up. The relationship between file size and bitrate is basically proportional, but the same isn't true of sound quality, so a 128 Kbps track takes half as much space as the same track recorded at 256 Kbps, but the sound will be only very marginally different. Still, marginal differences are what being a hi-fi obsessive is all about.

The default import setting in recent versions of iTunes, listed as "high quality", is AAC at 128 Kbps. Most people will be perfectly satisfied with this combination (which is usually said to be roughly equivalent to MP3 at 160 Kbps), but if you're into your sound in a serious way it may not be quite good enough. Particularly if you listen to high-fidelity recordings of acoustic instruments, such as well-recorded classical music, and if you connect your iPod or computer to a decent home stereo (see p.119), you may find AAC 128 Kbps leads to a distinct lack of presence and brightness in your favourite recordings. If so, either opt for the Apple Lossless Encoder (see p.105) or stick with AAC and up the bitrate. The best thing to do is to run a comparative experiment with a suitably well-recorded track (see box below).

Running a soundcheck

The only reliable way to determine the right sound quality for your own ear, headphones and hi-fi is to do a comparative experiment. Launch iTunes and insert a CD you consider to be as detailed and clear in its recording quality as anything in your collection. Pick one track that sounds particularly hi-fi and uncheck the rest of the tracks. Name it "Soundcheck ALE" in the song list, since you will be importing this at CD quality using Apple Lossless Format. Open iTunes Preferences (from the iTunes or Edit menu) and select Apple Lossless from the dropdown. Import the track. Once it's done, return to the CD in the Source list, rename the track "Soundcheck 128 ACC", select the ACC 128 Kbps option from Preferences, and import the track again. Do this again at various other ACC and/or MP3 bitrates – say 160, 224 and 320 Kbps – each time renaming the track so it's easy to locate.

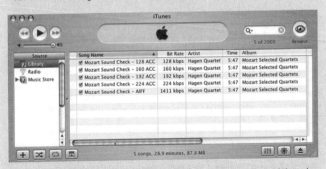

Once you're done, plug in your iPod, transfer the tracks across, and then do some comparative listening either on headphones or, ideally, connected through a decent home stereo and speaker system (see p.119). Then you can make an informed decision about what format is right for you.

Tweaking the settings

When setting the bitrate, the "Custom" option reveals a panel full of techie settings relating to frequencies and the like. You can safely ignore most of these, though it's worth knowing about one or two. Recording in mono (under channels) halves the file size, for example. And, if you're recording in MP3 format, explore the VBR –Variable Bitrate – feature. When switched on, the bitrate varies in real time, according to the complexity of the sound, potentially saving lots of disk space in the process.

WMA, Audible & Ogg Vorbis

Beside those formats listed on p.105, there are various others that you may come across – some of which iTunes and the iPod can handle and some of which they can't. Some of the most common are:

▶ **Windows Media** (.wma) If these have embedded DRM protection, iTunes won't touch them – unless you burn an audio CD of the tracks and re-rip it in another format. If, however, they're not DRM-protected, iTunes will simply create an AAC copy of them in your Library.

▶ **Audible** (.aa) This is a special format designed to sound good for spoken word – audio books, for example – at extremely low bitrates, but it isn't used for music. It's fully compatible with iTunes and iPods. For more, see p.140.

Terms like MP3 are so ubiquitous that it's easy to assume they're common property, but in fact nearly all such technologies are the intellectual assets of companies, which charge other companies (such as software manufacturers) to use them. Somewhere along the line, consumers foot the bill and profits may come before other considerations.

Increasingly, however, where there's a commercial piece of software there's also a free alternative produced by the open-source programming community (best known for the Linux operating system). And, true to form, the open-source crew have developed their own "patent-and-royalty-free" music format:

▶ **Ogg Vorbis** (.ogg) is claimed, by its designers, to sound better than any other (if you "dare to compare", visit www.vorbis.com). At the time of writing, Apple hasn't included Ogg Vorbis support into iTunes and the iPod. If you'd like to see them do so, drop Apple a line and let them know.

Re-encoding

iTunes allows you to change tracks easily from one format to another. This can sometimes be very useful: if you have any bulky WAV or AIFF files sitting around in your Library, for example, you can massively reduce the disk space they take up by converting them to Apple Lossless, AAC or MP3 format. And the resulting file will be as good as if you'd ripped it straight from CD. Be warned, however, that re-encoding files that are already in MP3, AAC or some other compressed format is in general a very bad idea. Each file format works by removing different things from the sound file, so even if MP3 and AAC both sound great, a track that has undergone both compressions may sound noticeably worse. You may sometimes think this is a price worth paying: if you have an archive of high-bitrate MP3s, for example, and you want to save disk space by reducing them to lower-bitrate AACs; or if you have a high-bitrate spoken-word recording that you're happy to reduce in quality. But before deleting the original versions be sure to carefully compare the sound through some decent headphones or a hi-fi and see if you're satisfied with the results.

To convert a track, first specify your desired format and bitrate under the Importing tab of Preferences, then select the file or

> ▶ **TIP: If you're a hi-fi buff with plenty of computer disk space, consider importing your CDs using Apple Lossless for use through your stereo (see p.119) but creating an AAC copy of each for use on your iPod, where disk space is more limited. After you've created the copies, simply create a Smart Playlist (see p.65) that finds all MP3 and AAC files, and set your Pod to automatically update that playlist only (see p.56).**

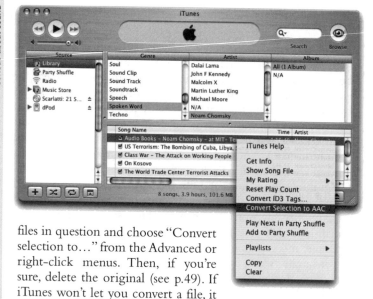

files in question and choose "Convert selection to…" from the Advanced or right-click menus. Then, if you're sure, delete the original (see p.49). If iTunes won't let you convert a file, it may have embedded DRM protection (see p.15). You may be able to get around this by putting the file on a standard audio CD (see p.88) and then re-ripping it in a different format. However, this may break the terms of your user licence, depending on where you got the track. The same is true of the various converting programs that you can easily find online. For more info, see www.mp3-converter.com

> **TIP: If you download and install an iTunes update, your import file format may default to Apple's AAC; if you prefer to import with a different format, change it back within Preferences under "Importing".**

10

Tweaking the sound

EQ and beyond

A s we've seen, one way to improve the sound on your computer and iPod is to be discerning with your import preferences (see p.104). Another option is to improve your speakers, either by investing in better earphones for your Pod (see p.179) or by hooking up to a decent hi-fi (see p.119). But aside from all this, you can also tweak the sound using various iTunes tools, including a pretty comprehensive graphic equalizer, which you can both apply as you listen and by assigning cusomized presets to different tracks, which then are transported to your iPod.

Preferences

The first port of call when dealing with sound in iTunes is the Preferences box (opened from the iTunes menu on a Mac or the Edit menu on a PC). Under Audio, there are two variables to be messed with.

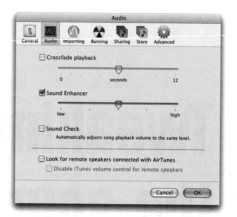

Sound Enhancer

In theory, when you set the Sound Enhancer to high you should notice a general improvement of the "presence" in the music you play. It's tricky to quantify, but the sound should be brighter and the stereo separation really vivid. You may not like the effect – or not be able to tell the difference – but it's certainly worth experimenting with, so check the box, slide the slider and see what you think.

Sound Enhancer is usually most beneficial for compressed audio formats like MP3 and AAC, but you may also notice a difference with CD playback. The only real downside is that it can keep your

Volume Adjustment

To boost or lower the volume of a particular track, select them in the song list and choose Get Info from the FIle menu. In the box that pops up, under Options, use the Volume Adjustment slider to alter the volume of that specific song. iTunes remembers the new setting and will use it whenever the song is played. You can do this for multiple tracks – or even whole genres, artists or albums in Browse mode (see p.47).

computer's processor pretty busy, which could result in glitches and skips if you don't have a fast machine.

Sound Check

When Sound Check is on, iTunes attempts to play back songs at approximately the same volume level, so you shouldn't have to keep turning the sound up and down as you jump around your collection. As more songs are added to your Library, iTunes recalculates its setting and stores the information in its database. It's not perfect, and you may still notice discrepancies in loudness between different songs, expecially where songs have been imported from a non-CD source. If particular tracks are still too quiet or loud, use the Volume Adjustment (see box opposite) setting to bring them into line.

A Rough Guide to EQ

All music, all sound in fact, is made up of vibrations at various different frequencies, which are expressed in hertz – cycles per second. Deep bass sounds are produced at low frequencies (as little as 32 hertz), while very high-pitched sounds come from much higher frequencies (perhaps 16 kilohertz, which means 16,000 cycles per second). All other audible sound lies somewhere in between.

Music, especially when produced by acoustic instruments, consists of an astonishingly complex and dynamic combination of different frequencies. And to get the optimum sound, you need to tweak the relative volume of the different frequencies according to your taste, your speakers, the recording quality and even the shape of a room you're in.

Most stereos offer the option to boost or suppress the loudness of high and low frequencies under the broad titles of "treble" and "bass". However, given that a range of frequencies could be divided into an infinite number of "bands", each of which could then be individually tweaked, there is scope for far more precision. In the world of hi-fi hardware, this precision is supplied by graphic equalizers, which offer a panel of sliders for adjusting the volume of various different frequency bands – changing the "EQ" of the overall sound. As explained overleaf, iTunes offers something very similar, but more flexible.

iTunes Equalizer

The iTunes Equalizer allows you to adjust a range of frequency bands (see the box on p.113) for the music coming out of your computer. To open Equalizer, hit its stripy button in the lower right corner of the iTunes pane.

> **TIP: On a Mac, you can also open Equalizer from the iTunes Window menu or by using the keyboard shortcut Apple+2.**

First make sure the Equalizer is active by checking the box in the top left of the pane. Note, though, that this window doesn't need to be open for the settings to be having an effect – you can tell whether the Equalizer is currently active by seeing whether its button in the main iTunes window is glowing blue.

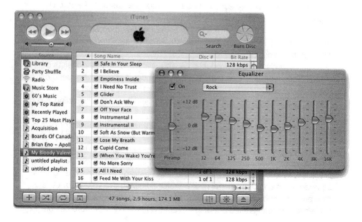

Presets

From the dropdown menu you can choose between a number of preset frequency settings, designed to suit different types of music: the "Dance" preset, for example, has a heavier bass setting, while the "Spoken Word" setting features stronger midrange frequencies, just like the human voice. Play some music that you are familiar with and try a few of the presets, even ones that don't sound at all suitable from their name. Take a look at the different shapes that the Equalizer's sliders make on-screen and get a feel for what is happening to the music. Toggle the tick box in the Equalizer panel "on" and "off" to compare your new settings to the unequalized version of the song.

Make your own presets

At any time you can drag the sliders up and down yourself to try and get a sound perfectly matched to the music you're listening to (as you do so, the Preset dropdown will display Manual). If you create an EQ that you like, you can save it by selecting "Make

serious about sound

Preset…" from the dropdown and choosing a name.

Once you've made a preset, you can recall its particualr combination of levels by clicking its entry in the dropdown menu. Or

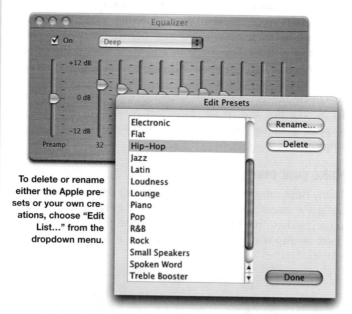

To delete or rename either the Apple presets or your own creations, choose "Edit List…" from the dropdown menu.

> **TIP:** If boosting individual frequency bands with the Equalizer causes the sound to distort, lower the Preamp setting to between −6db and −12db, and then compensate by increasing your computer's master volume level.

you can edit or rename the presets, as shown below.

116

> **TIP:** When constructing your own EQ presets, start with the "Flat" preset and build on that: you'll get a much better feel for the effect each of your additional drags is having on the original sound.

EQing songs

So far we've looked at using the Equalizer as a real-time tool, simply changing the settings and presets as we listen. But iTunes can do more than that: using the song information panels the program allows you to associate preset EQs with individual songs so that both iTunes and your iPod know exactly how you want to hear them.

First, in the song list select the song, or songs, you want to add an EQ preset to and then choose "Get Info" from the File menu. Now simple choose the preset you want to use from the Equalizer Preset drop-down menu (found under Options when you are dealing with a single song).

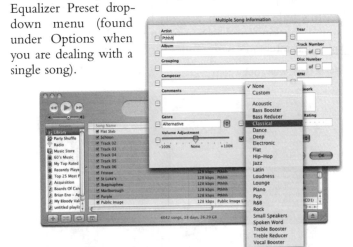

And on to the Pod...

All your Equalizer presets and individual song associations are carried over to the iPod when you update, though you can manually select the preset you want to use from the EQ menu within the iPod's main Settings menu. This is also the place to go to toggle the iPod's Sound Check function "on" and "off". However, the single best way to improve the sound that comes out of your iPod is to buy a good pair of sound-isolating head-phones (see p.179).

Third party plug-ins

The iTunes sound features are good, but if you want even more you'll find plenty of free or inexpensive programs on the Net. Among the best is Volume Logic. Available for both Mac and PC, this little application presents level meters, a plethora of "sound checking" and EQing functions, and a handsome little panel that integrates with iTunes very snuggly.

Volume Logic www.octiv.com

Hooking up to hi-fis

playing through ... recording from

The iPod does an excellent job of putting your music collection in your pocket. But when you want to listen at home, a pair of earphones is not what you want. Neither, for that matter, are tinny little computer speakers. The ideal solution is to hook up your iPod, your computer, or both, to a decent hi-fi – something that can be done in a number of ways. And, besides the obvious advantages in sound quality, marrying your computer and hi-fi also allows you to get music from vinyl, cassette and radio into your iTunes Library and onto your Pod.

Playing through a hi-fi

To get the sound from your Pod or computer into your hi-fi, the latter should ideally have an available line-in channel – look on the back for an unused pair of red and white RCA sockets. They may be labelled "Aux" or "Line-in", though any input other than Phono (which will have a built-in pre-amp) should be fine.

If your hi-fi doesn't have a line-in, but it does have a radio, you could consider an FM transmitter (see p.122). If it does have a line-in, you have a number of options…

Connecting with cables

Computer to hi-fi

Nearly all computers have line-out and/or headphone sockets (usually 3.5mm "minijack" sockets, but some computers have RCA line outs). So if your computer and stereo share a desk or are only a few metres apart, you can easily pick up an RCA-to-mini-jack cable (pictured), or an RCA-to-RCA cable, and run it straight from either of these sockets on your computer to the hi-fi's line-in.

When buying a cable, check all the plugs are "male" not "female" (they probably will be) and, if you can, spend a little extra to get gold-plated jacks – they deliver a far cleaner sound.

If your computer and hi-fi are further apart or in different rooms, you could buy a long cable and get the drill out, but you might prefer to investigate Airport Express (see p.122).

> **TIP:** If no signal seems to be getting to your stereo from iTunes, make sure that your volume is turned up both in the program and on your system's master volume.

iPod to hi-fi

One problem with running your computer through your hi-fi is that you need to have your computer on to hear anything, which can be a pain if your machine takes ages to boot up or has a noisy cooling fan. You might find it more convenient to attach your iPod instead. A Pod doesn't give you quite the ease of use and flexibility of iTunes, but it's small, silent and doesn't require you to run a cable across your room.

Simply run an RCA-to-minijack cable between your hi-fi's line-in and your Pod's headphone socket or, much better, the "Line Out" on the back of the Dock, as pictured here. The Dock solution can be made all the more convenient when combined with a wireless remote control (see p.174).

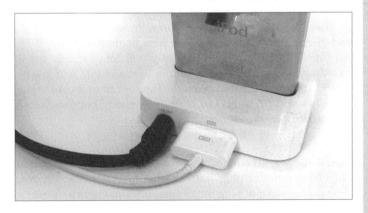

Connecting wirelessly

AirTunes

If your hi-fi has a line-in socket, but you don't want to be limited by cables – perhaps you have a laptop or your computer is in a different room to your stereo – investigate Apple's Airport Express wireless base station (pictured), with its so-called AirTunes feature.

Attach one of these to a power point near to your hi-fi and connect it to the stereo with a standard RCA-to-mini-jack cable. Then, any computer with Wi-Fi capability – known as AirPort on a Mac – can beam music straight from iTunes to the hi-fi, even from the other side of the house. If your computer doesn't have Wi-Fi you can add it inexpensively with the appropriate internal, external or PCMCIA device (see *The Rough Guide to the Internet* for more). Once everything's in place, you can simply open iTunes Preferences and check "Look for remote speakers connected with AirTunes" in the Audio tab. Your hi-fi will automatically appear in a dropdown menu on the bottom of the iTunes window.

Airport Express can also beam the Internet around your house, and allow you to connect to printers wirelessly. For more information, see: www.apple.com/airportexpress

FM transmitters

This is the way to connect if you lack a line-in on your stereo. An FM transmitter plugs into the headphone socket on your iPod (many will also plug into a computer) and beams the sound around the room as an FM radio signal. Then your stereo can tune in just as it would any other radio station. You won't get CD fidelity and your stereo or iPod will need to be relatively close to your radio. For more, see p.172.

> **TIP: As well as connecting to your home hi-fi, it's possible to connect to the one in your car. For more on this, see p.172 and p.177.**

Recording music from a hi-fi

Other than playing music through a home stereo speaker system, the other reason you might want to connect your computer to a hi-fi is to "rip" analogue sound sources (vinyl, cassettes, even a radio programme) into a digital file format. You can't record directly into the iPod this way, but anything you record onto your computer can then be transferred onto your Pod.

First of all, you'll need to make the right connection. With any luck, your computer will have a line-in or mic port, probably in the form of a minijack socket (if it doesn't you can add on with the right USB device; see box overleaf). On the hi-fi, a head-phone socket will suffice, but you'll get a much better "level" if your hi-fi has a dedicated line-out – check on the back for a pair of RCA sockets labelled "Line Out", "Tape Out" or something similar. That way, also, you'll only need a standard RCA-to-

> **TIP: You're not limited to household stereos. With the right cable you can record from any device with a headphone jack – including Walkmans, MiniDisc players and portable radios.**

Audio interfaces

Though most computers do feature line-in sock-ets, some – such as Apple's iBook – don't. But there are loads of pieces of USB hardware on the market that will provide you with a basic line-in and mic-in socket (such as Griffin's iMic, pictured) or, if your budget allows, a more professional selection of studio-quality ports and sockets.

iMic www.griffintechnology.com/products/imic

For insight, advice and details and reviews of other possibilities, try:

PC Music Guru (PCs and Macs) www.pcmusic.com
SilentWay.com (Macs) www.silentway.com/tips

minijack cable – which you might even already have.

Note that you'll need up to around a gig of hard drive space to record an album from vinyl or cassette. However, once you've finished you can convert the file to a much smaller MP3 or AAC track and delete the giant original.

Software

The other part of the equation is the software. You may already have something suitable on your system, but there are scores of excellent programs available to download off the Net. Here are few recommendations:

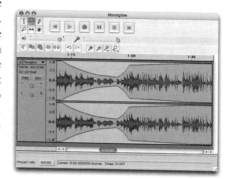

▶ **Audacity (Mac & PC)** With Audacity you can record and edit WAV, AIFF, Ogg Vorbis and MP3 files, and more. As well as built-in effects it features an unlimited undo function – very useful. Best of all, it's free.
http://audacity.sourceforge.net

▶ **AudioGrabber (PC)** This excellent freeware features normalizing (see p.126) and sound-enhancing tools. Supports Ogg Vorbis among others.
www.audiograbber.com

▶ **Auqio Sound Studio (PC)** Though it costs around $100, this program offers a plethora of recording and editing tools.
www.auqio.com

▶ **CD Spin Doctor (Mac)** Part of Roxio's CD-burning package Toast (roughly $80/£50), Spin Doctor allows you to record audio, clean and enhance sound quality, and create MP3 files ready to slip into iTunes.
www.roxio.com/toast

For many more options, including freebies, try:

AudioMelody www.audiomelody.com
Shareware Music Machine www.hitsquad.com/smm
Tucows www.tucows.com/audio_recorders_pop.html

> TIP: Audio-editing software also lets you trim, cut up or edit tracks in your iTunes Library – useful if you only want part of a big MP3.

Start recording

Overleaf you'll find a basic step-by-step guide to ripping from vinyl and other sources. But the finer details of recording and editing audio take a lifetime to master, so if you want good results, or you get stuck, do some reading online, starting with:

OSXAudio www.osxaudio.com
PC Music Guru www.pc-music.com

Mastering from vinyl – in five easy steps

Getting vinyl – or any other analogue format, for that matter – into your iTunes Library is more time-consuming than ripping from CD. You have to set the levels right, record the album or track in "real time", and then mess around with filters and effects to clean up your recordings.

The details vary according to which program you're running, but roughly speaking the procedure is the same:

1. Connect your stereo and hi-fi as described above, and switch your hi-fi's amp to "Phono".

2. Launch your audio recorder (see previous page) and open a new file. You'll be asked to specify a few parameters for the new recording. The defaults (usually 44.1 KHz, 16-bit stereo) should be fine. Play the loudest section of the record to get an idea of the maximum level. A visual meter should display the sound coming in – you want as much level as possible *without* hitting the red. If you seem to be getting little or no level, make sure your line-in is specified as your recording channel and the input volume is up: on a Mac, look under Sound in System Preferences; on a PC, check the line-in in Sound and Multimedia in the Control Panel, and the level by opening Volume Controls (Start Menu/Programs/Accessories/Entertainment), clicking Properties in the Options menu, selecting Recording and pressing OK.

3. When you are ready, press "Record" and then set your vinyl spinning. When the song or album's finished, press "Stop". A wave will appear on the screen. Use the "cut" tool to tidy up any extraneous noise or blank space from the beginning and end of the file; fade in and out to hide the "cuts".

4. If your software offers hiss, pop and crackle filters, give them a go, but don't overwrite your original file until you get the right sound – removing hiss and crackle is good, but if you end up with a recording that lacks the warmth or presence of the shellac version, you'll be disappointed. If there's a "normalize" function you could use this to maximize the level without distorting it.

5. When you are happy with what you've got, save it and perhaps back it up to CD. Then import the file into iTunes (choose "Import..." from the File menu), convert it to a compressed format of your choice (see p.109) and delete the bulky original from both your iTunes folder (see p.49) and it's original location.

MUSIC
ONLINE

12

iTunes Music Store

the Apple option

A s the following chapter shows, the iTunes Music Store isn't the only option for downloading music. But if you use iTunes and an iPod, it's unquestionably the most convenient, offering you instant, legal, access to hundreds of thousands of tracks for 99¢/79p each. Unlike some of its competitors, the iTunes Music Store is not a website, so don't expect to reach it with Internet Explorer or Safari. The only way in is through iTunes: simply connect to the Net, click the Music Store icon in the Source list, and after a few seconds the iTunes window will be taken over by the store's front page.

music online

Logging in for the first time

Though anyone can browse the iTunes Music Store, listen to samples and look at artwork to their heart's content, if you actually want to buy anything you need to set up an account.

If you already have either a .mac account or an AOL account (America only) you can sign in using your existing ID and password – simply click the account "Sign In" button in the top right corner of the iTunes window, enter your log-in details and hit "Sign In". If this is the first time you have used the Store

Sign In to buy music on the iTunes Music Store
To create an Apple Account, click Create New Account.

(Create New Account)

If you have an Apple Account (from the Apple Store or .Mac, for example), enter your Apple ID and password. Otherwise, if you are an AOL member, enter your AOL screen name and password.

○ 🍎   Apple ID:
                                              Example: steve@mac.com
                Password:
○ 🅰️ AOL   (Forgot Password?)

(?)   (Cancel) (Sign In)

> ▶ **TIP: Only one person can be logged in to the store from your computer at any one time. If someone else is already signed in you'll see their Apple ID in the Account button. Click the button, then click "Sign Out" and log in as normal.**

you will need to verify your account and payment details on-screen before you can start buying and downloading.

If you don't already have any account details, hit the "Sign In" button (top right), then "Create New Account", and follow the prompts to enter your payment and contact details. After only a few minutes you'll be ready to start browsing and buying.

You'll need your ID and password whenever you visit the Store, so keep a record of it. But keep it safe.

> ▶ **TIP: To view your account details at any time, click your account name button in the top right corner of the store's pane, enter your password and then hit "View Account".**

Apple Store DRM

The songs sold by the Music Store are AAC files protected by DRM (see p.15), which means there are certain encoded restrictions that control what you can actually do with them. At the time of writing, these restrictions are:

▶ Your downloads can only be played on five "authorized" computers at any one time. However, you can change which computers these are.

▶ You can burn individual purchased songs to CD as many times as you like, you can only burn a playlist seven times if it contains purchased songs (you can always recompile the playlist).

What have they got?

At the time of writing, the iTunes Music Store boasts in excess of 700,000 songs and more than 5000 audiobooks, and the list is growing all the time. However, the Store is not like a regular record shop where anything can be ordered if you want it: as with any download site, anything that's up there is the result of a deal struck with the record label in question. There are still a lot of glaring catalogue omissions, and many independent record distributors have flatly refused to sign up – so don't expect to find everything you want.

That said, thousands of new tracks appear week after week, so the situation can only get better. And there are plenty of other places to look if you can't find what you want – see p.137.

Navigation

You shouldn't struggle to find your way around the iTunes Music Store. Like online CD stores such as Amazon, it lets you puruse by genre, look at "Staff Favourites", "Featured Artists", "Exclusives" and so on. But it also let's you use the various tools familar from browsing your own iTunes Library.

Searching

Once you are in the Store the iTunes Search field (see p.49) can be used to search the Store's catalogue. The homepage also features a link to "Power Search" where you can further narrow your search criteria.

> ▶ TIP: Use the Apple key (Mac) or Ctrl key
> (Windows) in conjunction with the square-
> bracket keys to go back and forth between
> Music Store windows.

Browsing

The browse function works in exactly the same way as it does for your own Library (see p.47): hit the "Browse" button in the top right corner and then browse genres, artists and albums in the columns that appear.

You can go "up a level", or right back to the Store's homepage, by clicking the tabs at the top right.

Quicklinks

Whether you are browsing your own Library or the Music Store's catalogue, you can use the grey circular Quicklink buttons in the song list to quickly access all the Music Store's selections for a particular artist. Quicklinks can be turned on and off for your own Library in iTunes Preferences under General.

Previewing music

You can preview thirty seconds' worth of any track within the Music Store catalogue simply by double-clicking the song's name in the song list. You can also drag any previews into playlists on the Source list to listen to later. These previews will appear in the song list all ready for you to click when you want to buy the whole track.

Buying music

Once you're ready to buy some tracks, there are two ways to go about it. You could use the "1-Click" method whereby a single click of a "Buy Song" button in the song list will debit the payment from your card and start the track downloading to your iTunes Library.

Alternatively you can shop using a "Shopping Cart", which appears in the Source list. As you browse the store you add songs to your cart using the "Add Song" buttons; when you are done, click the cart's icon in the Source list, inspect its contents and then hit the "Buy Now" button in the bottom right corner to pay and start downloading.

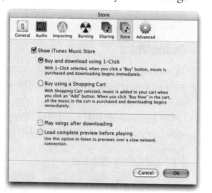

You can set which method you wish to use in the iTunes Preferences panel under "Store".

Authorizing your computer

Music purchased from the iTunes Music Store can only be "Authorized" for use on five machines at any one time. This way Apple hope that they can curb the unauthorized sharing of copyrighted music. Your computer is authorized to play music you purchase when you set up your account, or when you enter your ID and password to play a song that you purchased.

If your account is already authorized with five computers, you will have to deauthorize one of the machines before playing music on a sixth. This is done by selecting "Deauthorize computer..."

from the Advanced menu in iTunes. Equally, if you ever plan to sell or ditch an old machine which has been used to play purchased songs, make sure you deauthorize it before you say goodbye.

What else?

Publish an iMix

The iTunes Music Store also gives you the option of publishing your own playlists within the Store so that others can either draw inspiration from (or snigger at) your impeccable taste. To publish a playlist, either click the arrow link to the right of the playlist in the Source list or choose "Create an iMix…" from the File menu. Only songs available in the Music Store will be published in the iMix.

To email a friend with the link to your published iMix, click the arrow button to the right of the published playlist in the Source list, and then click "Tell a friend".

The gift of music

If you are feeling generous you can use your Music Store to buy and send "Gift Certificates" that can be redeemed in the store; the link is on the homepage with full instructions. Here you'll also see a link for

setting up a "Monthly Gift" allowance account: you authorize someone to spend a set amount of money each month that is then charged to your credit card.

Billboard charts

If you are a patron of the US iTunes Music Store there is also a link on the homepage to the *Billboard* charts, and not just their current listing, but hit parades from years gone by – pure nostalgia. (You can choose to browse the US Store from Europe via the dropdown menu at the bottom of the homepage.)

Freebies

Keep an eye open for free tracks: you get something for nothing, and you might discover something you never knew you liked. Also on offer are free-to-stream music videos, though you'll need a fast Internet connection to make them worth watching.

TIP: Just like any other item in the Source list, double-clicking the Music Store's icon opens it in a separate window.

13

More music online

buying music online

Though it's the obvious choice for iTunes users, the iTunes Music Store doesn't hold all the cards when it comes to selling music online. There are many other services out there. Some of them are less expensive than iTunes; others offer tracks that iTunes doesn't; and some even donate their profits to charity. We've covered the full range over the next few pages to give you an idea of what's out there, but, as we explain, many of these aren't immediately compatible with iTunes or the iPod.

music online

Compatibility

Since the advent of DRM (see p.15), you can't simply download a song from any site or service and play it back in any jukebox or digital music player. It depends on the type of DRM and also the file types supported by the software and hardware in question.

Though DRM for MP3 files has only recently been developed, in almost all cases if you find an MP3 file you'll be able to play it back in iTunes and on the iPod – and do anything else you want with it. But increasingly the music available legally online takes the form of DRM-protected WMA files, which are designed to play back on Windows Media Player and not currently compatible with either iTunes or the iPod. And this situation looks unlikely to change any time soon, since Apple are inevitably keen to keep people shopping at the iTunes Music Store rather than any of its competitors.

It is possible to get around the compatibility issue. If the DRM on a track doesn't stop you burning it to CD, you can always try doing just that and then re-ripping the same track in a format that iTunes can handle. You may also find software online that can strip the protection away. And there's always the option of playing back the file while re-recording it with an audio editor (see p.124). However, none of these options will do wonders for the sound quality, and it may well break the terms of your licence agreement. For more on DRM, see: www.drmwatch.com

> The majority of music downloading these days takes place via file-sharing networks. These make it easy and quick to get hold of just about anything you want, but downloading copyrighted music from them is against the law. For more on file-sharing, see p.143.

Despite all this, there are quite a few sites that offer legal MP3s and other files compatible with iTunes and the iPod. Many of these are smaller, more specialized companies focusing on a particular style – including those areas not currently well served by Apple's own music store. Audio Lunchbox, for example, offers an excellent selection of tracks from indie labels. Bleep gives you access to lots of electronica that you won't find elsewhere – at least not legally. And Calabash Music serves up world music according to fair-trade principles. These are all straightforward online stores, accessible with a Web browser:

Audio Lunchbox www.audiolunchbox.com
Bleep www.bleep.com
Calabash Music www.calabashmusic.com

But others cover all genres. In the UK, for example, Wippit offers MP3 (as well as WMA) downloads for as little as 29p per track or £50 per year for an unlimited number. The selection is smaller but less mainstream than that at iTunes.

Wippit www.wippit.com

And there are a number of sites which offer access to free music by amateur or up-and-coming artists. These include PeopleSound and CNet's Download.com Music. It holds the archive that used to live at MP3.com – now a site that lets you compare (and search for tracks across) the major music service.

Download.com Music http://music.download.com
MP3 www.mp3.com
PeopleSound www.peoplesound.com

As for spoken word, though the iTunes Music Store offers many audio books, the best

audible.com®
audio that speaks to you *wherever* you are

place to shop is Audible.com, where you'll find tens of thousands of offerings – from language primers to modern fiction. You can either become a member and pay a monthly subscription or buy books individually.

Audible.com www.audible.com

The big guns

Following is a brief run-through of the major music services out there offering competition to iTunes. These big guns are the ones which – at the time of writing, at least – won't officially work with iTunes or an iPod. Many of them also won't work on a Mac. Still, PC users might be interested to check them out – perhaps to use them alongside iTunes. The services fall into two main categories: pay-per-track and subscriptions.

Pay-per-track

iTunes' main competitors in the pay-per-track department include, in the US, BuyMusic, which offers selections for as little as 79¢ each, and Musicmatch (see p.184), who provides a similar service to iTunes but with a more Windows-style feel.

In Europe, various suppliers offer the hundreds of tracks supplied by OD2 (see box, p.142). These include Oxfam's Big Noise Music, from which profits go towards fighting world poverty.

And on both sides of the Atlantic, there's Sony's Connect.

Penny jukebox

Sonic Selector offer an online music jukebox service. For 1p per track songs can be streamed (but not downloaded) from a library of more than 350,000 songs, so it's a little like having an instant online record collection.
At the time of writing, the Sonic Selector is only available in Europe as a Windows Media Player Series 9 plug-in for the PC and comes as a branded package through either MSN, Tiscali, Packard Bell or MTV.

Sonic Selector www.sonicselector.com

Big Noise Music www.bignoisemusic.com (Europe; PC only)
BuyMusic www.buymusic.com (US; PC & Mac)
Connect www.connect.com (US & Europe; PC only)
Musicmatch www.musicmatch.com (US; PC only)

Subscription services

The main legal alternative to paying per track is to sign up with a subscription service. Each one works differently, but in general your monthly fee will get you unlimited hi-fi streaming (which requires broadband) and, usually, a set number of downloads. Check the fine print before you sign up.

Somewhat ironically, the major players include Napster, reborn as a legitimate business after being shut down as an illegal file-sharing service. It now boasts one of the largest catalogues of tracks – over 700,000 songs in its UK branch alone. But they're only one of many such services:

eMusic's Rapsody www.emusic.com (US; PC & Mac)
Listen www.listen.com (US; PC only)
MusicNet (AOL) www.musicnet.com (US; PC & Mac)
Napster www.napster.com (US, Can & UK; PC only)
Streamwaves www.streamwaves.com (US; PC only)
Vitaminic www.vitaminic.co.uk (International; PC & Mac)

Different sites ... same music

There are scores of sites and services offering music streams and downloads, but many are basically retailing access to the archives of a music wholesaler. In the US, for example, Lycos and Listen.com are supplied by the Real network's **Rhapsody** (www.real.com/rhapsody), while in Europe **OD2** (www.ondemanddistribution.com) serves many of the major services.

And more...

There are loads of other sites offering both pay-to-download legal MP3s and free previews. Some more to explore...

ClickMusic www.clickmusic.co.uk
Dmusic www.dmusic.com
Epitonic www.epitonic.com
IUMA www.iuma.com
Launch.com www.launch.com
Liquid Audio www.liquid.com

These days most of the contraband is traded via file-sharing networks (see p.143) but you may also come across some on the Web, especially if you visit an MP3 search engine, such as:

Lycos http://music.lycos.com

In between the legit and the illegit, there are MP3 websites that are, well, kind of legal. All Of MP3, for example, is the best-known of the Russian sites that use a loophole in their country's broadcast law to openly offer a huge download archive without permission from the labels. They offer all formats and bitrate "by the weight" – you buy, say, 100 MB for a comparatively tiny fee. It's left up to you to ensure you don't break the law of your own country when downloading.

All Of MP3 www.allofmp3.com

14

P2P file sharing

legalities & practicalities

While the iTunes Music Store may have competition from other commercial download services, it's probably fair to sat that its primary competitor is P2P file sharing, a technology that allows computer users all over the world to "share" each other's files – including music files – via the Internet. Even if you've never heard of P2P ("peer-to-peer") you've probably heard of some of the programs that have made this kind of file sharing possible, such as KaZaA and, historically speaking, Napster. And you've probably also heard people debating the legal and moral ins and outs of the free-for-all that file-sharing programs facilitate. If not, don't worry – the next few pages will bring you up to speed.

The basics

On a home or office network, it's standard for users of each computer to have some degree of access to the files stored on the other computers. P2P file-sharing programs apply this idea to the whole of the Internet – which is, of course, simply a giant network of computers. In short, anyone who installs a P2P program can access the "shared folder" of anyone else running a similar program. And these shared folders are mostly filled with high-quality MP3 music files.

With literally millions of file sharers online at any one time, an unthinkably large quantity of music is up there. And it's not just music: any file can be made available, from video and images to software and documents. So, whether you're after a drum'n'bass track, a website-design application, a Chomsky speech or an episode of *Friends*, you're almost certain to find it. But that doesn't mean that it's legal. If you download or make available any copyright-protected material, you are breaking the law and, while it's still currently unlikely, you could in theory be prosecuted.

The legal battle

Continuous legal action saw Napster – the first major P2P system – bludgeoned into submission (it has now resurfaced as one of the larger legitimate online music providers; see p.141). A similar fate befell Scour, this time because of movie rather than audio sharing. But these casualties just paved the way for the many alternatives, of which the most popular has proved to be KaZaA, which now stands by some margin as the most downloaded program in the history of the Internet.

So far, despite their not inconsiderable efforts, the music, film and software companies have failed to put an end to this new-generation file sharing. Mainly this is because, unlike the old

iP2P?

The market position of iTunes and the iPod is often said to be strengthened by the wide range of third-party software and accessories available for it. But among these are programs that must make Apple – who are eager to get on the right side of the music industry – cringe. It was only a matter of time, for example, before someone developed a program to turn the Mac version of iTunes into a file-sharing program, allowing users around the globe to browse and download the Libraries of others. That program was iCommune (www.icommune.net), though legal wranglings seem to have stopped it taking the Net by storm.

programs, the new ones create a genuinely decentralized network: they don't rely on a central system to keep tabs on which files are where. Which means that, even though the programs are mostly used for the illegal distribution of copyrighted material, the companies producing them can't easily be implicated in this breach of the law (just as a knife manufacturer couldn't easily be sued for a stabbing involving their product).

Instead, the music industry, led by the US trade body RIAA has gone after the people who clearly *are* breaking the law: individual file sharers downloading or making available copyrighted material. Quite a few individuals have now been prosecuted – in the US, at least – creating a major backlash of public opinion against RIAA. But with many millions of people using file sharing each day, it's pretty inconceivable that the company would be able to go after every one of them.

Whether or not it's ethical to use P2P to download copyrighted material for free, however, is another question. Some people justify it on the grounds that they use file sharing as a way to listen to new music they're considering buying on CD; others claim they refuse to support a music industry that, in their view, is doing more harm than good; other still that they

music online

only download non-controversial material, such as recordings of speeches, for example. It's a heated debate – as is the question of whether file sharing has damaged legal music sales, something the industry insists upon, but which many experts claim is questionable.

For both sides of the argument, see:

EFF www.eff.org/share
RIAA www.riaa.org

How it works

Though all P2P file sharing takes place via the Internet, there are various discrete "networks", or protocols. The main ones, in alphabetical order, are eDonkey2000, FastTrack, Gnutella, OpenNap and WinMX. They're all huge and most are accessible via various different programs ("clients"), many of which are very sophisticated, with features such as the ability to download a single file from more than one source (which speeds things up and avoids dropout). Many also have built-in media players or even the ability to import downloaded tracks directly into a special playlist in iTunes. However, some programs are also riddled with spyware and adware – something long associated with KaZaA, for example.

Multi-network clients

There are now clients available for both PC and Mac that trawl some or all of the major networks for results. For example:

iSwipe www.hillmanminx.net/swipe (Mac only)
MLDonkey www.nongnu.org/mldonkey (PC & Mac)
Morpheus www.morpheus.com (PC only)
XNap http://xnap.sourceforge.net (PC only)

Below is a list of major networks and some of the most popular programs for accessing them. All of these can be downloaded and be used for free, though some nag users to make a donation to the developer or pay for a more fully featured, ad-free version (Grokster Pro, for example, costs $30). Note that new programs come out all the time, as do upgrades of the exisiting ones.

FastTrack

Thanks to the success of KaZaA, this is currently the largest network, so has been the focus of much of the legal battle. Other than KaZaA, applications for accessing this network include Grokster, iMesh and, for the Mac, the multi-network iSwipe application (see box).

Grokster www.grokster.com (PC only)
iMesh www.imesh.com (PC only)

eDonkey2000 and Overnet

The eDonkey2000 network can be accessed via the original eDonkey program, but the newer eMule has more features. The people behind eDonkey also set up the Overnet network, originally intended as a replacement for eDonkey2000: both now have their own clients, which feed off each other's networks, and both are still growing. Mac users are catered for by MLDonkey, a client that can also be used to access the FastTrack network.

eDonkey2000 www.edonkey2000.com (PC only)
eMule www.emule-project.net (PC only)
MLDonkey www.nongnu.org/mldonkey (PC & Mac)
Overnet www.overnet.com (PC only)

Gnutella and Gnutella 2

Gnutella is a popular and well-stocked network accessible via a wide range of very usable programs, such as Acquisition, Gnucleus, LimeWire, Morpheus, XoloX and the feature-packed Shareaza.

Acquisition www.acquisition.com (Mac only)
Gnucleus www.gnucleus.com (PC only)
LimeWire www.limewire.com (Mac only)
Morpheus www.morpheus.com (PC only)
Shareaza www.shareaza.com (PC only)
XoloX www.xolox.nl (PC only)

Acquisition

WinMX and OpenNap

Though not as user-friendly as some programs, WinMx accesses the post-Napster OpenNap network as well as its own WinMX network. Between them, these include a truly huge amount of music.

WinMX www.winmx.com (PC only)

More

There are many other programs and networks out there (as well as other ways of sharing files, such as newsgroups and chat). But don't download just any program or you may end up with spyware in your system. For reviews of all the available programs, plus news and links to download sites, see:

Mac-P2P.com www.mac-p2p.com
Slyck www.slyck.com
ZeroPaid www.zeropaid.com

15

Internet radio

tuning in online

Radio on the Internet works pretty much like radio in the real world, except that – what with the Net being global and there being no online equivalent to radio stations fighting over frequency bands – the choice is almost infinite. You're limited neither by your geographical area nor your next door neighbour's four-storey gazebo. You can listen to a fair selection of radio stations within iTunes, but, as we explain, this is only a tiny fraction of what's available elsewhere on the Net.

Online radio and the law

You may wonder how so much music can be available online for free, and the answer lies in the fact that it is streamed, not downloaded. Back in the mid-90s when companies like Napster were busy fighting in the courts, Internet radio was flourishing, and legal, thanks to a loophole in American law that exempted "non-interactive, non-downloadable" digital media from licence fees. By the end of the 90s the law had tightened and demands for enormous licence fees almost destroyed the blossoming Internet radio scene, forcing streams to become pirate stations.

Thankfully, a "Small Webcasters Amendment Act" imposed more realistic licence fee levels based on audience size, and the legal Net radio is thriving. However, programs that allow you to "rip" streaming audio to your hard drive (see p.152) are raising legal eyebrows.

Radio in iTunes – and on the iPod

Radio in iTunes is extremely simple. Make sure your machine is connected to the Internet, click the Radio icon in the Source list and browse through the list of musical genres that appears in the song list, clicking the triangle

 TIP: You can create shortcuts to your favourite stations by dragging them into a playlist in the Source list.

> ▸ **TIP:** Programs such as iTunes "buffer" online
> radio, delaying the content for a few seconds
> so that, if there's a brief interruption in the
> stream, there's enough in reserve so that you won't
> notice. If your iTunes radio is prone to glitches, try
> increasing the "Streaming Buffer Size" to Large under
> the Advanced tab in iTunes' Preferences.

to the left of each genre to reveal a list of available stations.

For each station you'll also see a brief comment (which should give you an idea of what the station is all about) and a bitrate. The latter is important as you will only enjoy a glitch-free listening experience if you select stations which stream at a bitrate that is either equal to, or slower than, your Internet connection. If you surf with broadband you shouldn't have any problems with anything on offer, but if you're dialling up with a 56K modem stick to the low-bitrate stations.

When you've found a station you like the look of, double-click it, wait a few seconds, and the stream should begin. When you've had enough, either double-click another station or click Library in the Source list to return to your own collection.

New stations are frequently made available online, to check that your list is up-to-date, connect to the Internet, select Radio in the Source list and then hit the Refresh button in the top right corner of the iTunes window.

Onto the iPod

There are two main limitations with online radio, apart from the sometimes imperfect sound quality. One is that, though some online radio stations offer programmes "on demand", you generally have to be in the right place at the right time to listen to them. Second, you can't access online radio on your iPod.

However, there are programs available specifically for getting around these limitations by recording radio onto your hard drive as MP3 files. RadioLover (Mac) and HiDownload (PC), for example, allow you to set up schedules for recording the same show each day or week, record multiple streams simultaneously, and even break streams into individual MP3 files. However, depending on your country, the station you're listening to, and what you do with the download, recording from a radio stream may be illegal.

HiDownload www.hidownload.com
RadioLover www.bitcartel.com/radiolover

There are many other radio-related utilities out there, such as iTunes Radio Lover (not to be confused with RadioLover) which displays the artwork and title of the song currently streaming in iTunes, along with links to buy the track from Apple or Amazon.

iTunes Radio Lover www.widgetgallery.com/?category+5

Beyond iTunes...

As mentioned above, iTunes only scratches the surface of online radio. Search Google or browse a directory such as About, and you'll find links to thousands more stations.

About Radio http://radio.about.com

Most stations are accessed via a website. All you need to tune in, if you don't have them already, are the right media players: RealOne (there's a free version buried in the site) and Windows Media Player (available for Mac and PC).

RealOne www.real.com
Windows Media Player www.windowsmedia.com/download

MORE THAN MUSIC

16

iPod as
hard drive

transferring and backing up files

Though they might be revolutionizing the way we listen to music, iPods are, at the end of the day, little more than hard drives – just like the ones in our computers – in pretty little boxes. So it's no surprise that, besides its role as digital music player, an iPod can also function exactly like a standard external hard drive, storing any type of computer file. Assuming you have some free space on your Pod, you can use this feature for anything from backing up your photo archive to transporting documents between home and the office – even, on a Mac, rebooting your system after a major crash. And your Pod will still play music as usual.

Enabling hard drive use

To use your iPod as a hard drive, first you have to enable this feature. Simply attach the Pod to your computer as usual, and, when iTunes recognizes its presence, click its icon on the Source list and press the iPod Preference button at the bottom of the window (see p.55). Check the "Enable disk use" box and accept the warning about "manu-

iPod Preferences

⦿ Automatically update all songs and playlists
◯ Automatically update selected playlists only:

☐ 60's Music
☐ My Top Rated
☐ Recently Played
☐ Top 25 Most Played
☐ Acquisition

◯ Manually manage songs and playlists

☐ Open iTunes when attached
☑ Enable disk use
☐ Only update checked songs

(Cancel) (OK)

al unmounting" – it's only telling you that you'll have to press Eject when you've finished using it.

Using the iPod as a hard drive on Mac *and* PC

When you first plug your iPod into your computer, it prepares it for use by "formatting" the hard drive. iPods formatted on a PC can be recognized by both PCs and Macs, which is great if you're using your iPod as a hard drive, as it means you can move files between nearly all computers. However, iPods formatted on a Mac can only be recognized by Macs. So, if you intend to use your Mac-formatted iPod with both platforms – either to manually update music or transfer files – consider reformatting the Pod on a PC. This should only be done using the iPod Software Updater program, which will have come on a CD with the Pod. Before running the program, try checking the Apple website (see p.202) to see if a more up-to-date version is available to download. Then set it running and choose "Restore" (not "Update"). Note that this will delete all music, contacts and notes that the Pod contains – you'll have to move everything back onto it afterwards.

Using your new drive

Once disk use has been enabled, your iPod will appear as a standard drive (or volume), as well as within iTunes, whenever you connect it to your computer. On a Mac it appears on the Desktop and in the left-hand column of Finder windows (illustrated); in this state, the drive is said to be "mounted". On a PC it appears within My Computer as an external drive icon with a drive identification letter (perhaps "F:" or "G:").

Now you can use the drive as you would any other volume: within either Windows or OS X view its contents (though your music will be invisible), create folders, drag files on, drag files off. You'll probably find three folders in the iPod's drive when you open it: these relate to iPod organizer functions (see p.159) and shouldn't be deleted.

more than music

Ejecting your drive

When you are done with the drive, eject it (or "dismount" it) in the same way you would whenever the "Do not disconnect" message is displaying (see p.57).

One for Mac spods – the iPod startup disk

Do you own an iBook or PowerBook? Are you technically minded? Then you could try installing the recovery software that came with your Mac onto your iPod. This would give you a useful means of restarting and repairing your computer if it ever died when you were out and about and you didn't have the CDs to hand. You can even go the whole way and install a fully working OS to your Pod, though it may never play music again. Both these activities are beyond the scope of this book, but if you fancy giving it a go look online for tips and advice. Start with the iPod forums at...

iPodHead www.ipodhead.com
iPod Lounge www.ipodlounge.com

17

iPod as organizer

contacts, dates and wake-up calls

As a record collection in your pocket, the iPod is superb. As a portable hard drive, it's equally excellent. As an organizer, it's a bit more basic, and doesn't offer anything like the range of features of a proper PDA. Still, the functions it does have can certainly be useful. It can act as an address book, taking the contacts database from your computer's address book. It can display a calendar of appointments. And it can even wake you up in the morning with a musical playlist of your choice.

Contacts and calendars

Getting contacts onto your iPod from your computer – or even from a mobile phone – is not too difficult, assuming that you can export the contacts info, from wherever it currently lives, in the vCard format. Once you've done that, it's simply a matter of putting the vCards into the Contacts folder, which you'll find inside your iPod if you enable it as a hard drive (see p.155). Calendars, similarly, need to find their way into the iPod's Calendars folder in either the iCalendar or vCalendar format.

You can do all this manually by exporting the data from the relevant program and saving it onto the iPod, but it's far easier to use a syncing program. That way you don't need to worry too much about file formats and you know the iPod's lists of contacts and appointments will always be kept up-to-date. Here's a brief look at how you might do it from some common programs.

▶ **Address Book & iCal (Mac)**
Connect your iPod to your Mac and open the built-in iSync program from the OS X Applications folder. From the Devices menu choose "Add Device…" and, in the pane that pops up, double-click the icon for your Pod and then check the boxes for syncing your Address Book Contacts

and iCal calendars; you can additionally choose for this sync to take place every time your iPod is connected. Job done.

> **TIP: You can move individual calendars onto iPod manually. In iCal, select a calendar and choose "Export..." from the File menu. Save it to the Desktop and then drag it to the Calendars folder in your hard-disk-enabled Pod.**

▶ **Microsoft Outlook (PC)** Again, there are manual options, but it is far easier to download and use a program such as iPodSync or Pocket Mac (PC Edition). These applications can deal with Outlook's contacts, calendars, tasks and notes and they are very user-friendly. But note: they are only Outlook, not Outlook Express. Download the demo versions at…

iPodSync http://iccnet.50megs.com/ipodsync
Pocket Mac www.pocketmac.net

▶ **Microsoft Entourage (Mac)** Your best bet is to use the Mac version of Pocket Mac, which will run in tandom with iSync to transform your Entourage contacts, calendars, tasks, notes and even emails into an iPod-friendly format.

Pocket Mac www.pocketmac.net

▶ **Palm Desktop (Mac and PC)** Again, to get your list of contacts from the Palm Desktop Address Book, you could export the data in vCard format and manually plant it in the iPod's Contacts folder. A cleaner option, if you're using a Mac, is to let iSync deal with your Palm contacts. On a PC, try Palm2iPod:

Palm2iPod http://maxnoy.com/ipod

…on the iPod

Once all this information is safely aboard your Pod, browsing it is easy. From the top-level menu, select either "Contacts" or "Calendars" (if they aren't in the menu, head for the Settings menu and activate them under "Main Menu") and start browsing with the scroll wheel, clicking on dates of names that you want to see more details about.

In the Calendars menu you can set an alarm – either a beep or an on-screen text message – to alert you to any appointments to which an alarm setting has been assigned in the mother program.

The Calendars menu also offers access to the To Do menu, where tasks that have travelled over from your Mac or PC are stored.

> **TIP: Use the iPod's ⏮ and ⏭ buttons to skip back and forth between appointments within calendars.**

iPod clock and alarm clock

Select Clock from the iPod's top-level menu and you'll be presented with a handy little timepiece that also has an alarm feature. You can set the date, time and alarm time by selecting Date & Time from the Settings menu.

Here you can also choose whether you'd like to display the clock at the top of the iPod screen and, if you're using the alarm clock, how you'd like it to sound. The beep is audible, but only lasts for a few seconds, so don't rely on it to get you up in time for a job interview. Alternatively, you can choose to be woken up by a playlist of your choice but, unless you like to sleep wearing a pair of headphones, this will rely on you having your iPod hooked up to a stereo (see p.119) or external speakers. When the alarm is set a small bell appears on the right of the screen.

If you want to be woken up by music when travelling, consider a unit such as Griffin's iTalk (see p.170), which clips on the top of the iPod and boasts a a small but acceptable speaker.

> **TIP: If you want to use your computer as a musical alarm clock, download an iTunes controller with alarm clock features (see p.183).**

18

Notes, games & more

text docs, quizzes and voice memos

arly iPods featured a hidden breakout game, which could only be acessed with a "secret" sequence of button clicks – not that the secret lasted long, of course. On the current Pod models the games are easily accessed and, though Brick and Parachute ain't all that, the iPod's built-in Music Quiz is a winner. More useful, though, is the Notes feature, which allows you to read text docs of any type when you're out and about – or even have them read to you.

more than music

Notes

Once you've got your iPod enabled as a hard drive (see p.155), you can fill it with essays, novels or college work, among other things. But if you want to actually be able to read any of these word-based documents on your Pod you first have to save them in text-only format (with a .txt extension) and move them into the iPod's Notes folder.

All word processors will let you resave docs in simple text, or "ASCII", format. But don't save over your original file, as the plain-text version will strip out all formatting, such as colours, fonts and underlining. And note that if the resulting file is any bigger than 4k, you'll have to chop it up into smaller chunks in order to make it readable on the iPod.

> **Shall I compare thee to Apple's flagship hard-disk-based MP3 player?** Look online and you can find iPod-friendly versions of everything from the best of the Bard: www.westering.com/ipod

...via a Formula 1 encyclopedia:
www.kimistuff.com/ipod.html

...to the American Constitution:
www.acslaw.org/misc/iPoddl.htm

For more "podBooks", see:
www.ipodlibrary.com

iSpeak

If you find it annoying or impossible to read your text docs on the tiny screen of your iPod, why not have them read to you? Mac users can turn to iSpeak – a nifty little program that can turn written documents into spoken-word AAC files and inject them into your iTunes Library. It also features links to convert Google News, weather forecasts and the text from any webpage into a similar speech file, all ready for you to take out and about on your Pod. However, the program uses the computerized voice that you might have heard barking at you when an error message appears on screen – so don't expect a sympathetic interpretation of your favourite William Blake poem.

Fonix iSpeak does pretty much the same job for PC users.

iSpeak It (Mac) www.zapptek.com/ispeak-it
Fonix iSpeak www.fonix.com

You could also copy text from webpages or elsewhere, paste it into a word processor and resave the result as a text-only doc. However, you can find many ready-made "podBooks" online (see opposite) and there are even programs that will create Pod-readable text files automatically. iPodLibrary will convert eBooks in either the .pdf or .lit formats:

iPodLibrary www25.brinkster.com/carmagt/ipodlibrary

iPod It, meanwhile, will automatically download news, weather and the like from the Web and stick them on your Pod:

iPod It www.zapptek.com/ipod-it

Once a readable doc has been placed on your Pod, you can find it in the Notes menu (if it's not in the top-level menu, head for the Settings menu and activate it under "Main Menu"). Select the document you want to read, and use the scroll wheel to browse through the text. To delete text docs from your iPod, simply drag the files from the iPod Notes folder to the Trash (Mac) or Recycle Bin (PC).

more than music

Games

The games on the iPod can be found under the Games menu in the iPod's top-level menu (if the menu options is absent, it can be turned on in the Settings menu under "Main Menu").

There really isn't much to say about Brick, Solitaire and Parachute. They might keep you entertained for five minutes, but don't expect much – the iPod ain't no GameBoy.

The Music Quiz, on the other hand, is great fun. It randomly selects songs from your library and plays the first ten seconds. You have to try and spot the song from a list of five as quick as you can. It can be quite addictive.

Other things you can do with an iPod

Beside the functions we've outlined so far, the iPod can do a variety of extra jobs with the help of the appropriate third-party add-on. And design freaks and brand loyalists fear not – most iPod accessories are white and feature an "i" at the beginning of their name. Here are some ideas of what else you can do:

▶ Record a voice memo (see p.170).

▶ Download photos direct from your camera (see p.176).

▶ Interrupt an FM radio signal with a homemade newsflash (see p.172).

▶ Shave off your beard (see p.207).

EXTRAS

19

Accessories

plug and play

There are scores of iPod accessories available, from the obvious – cases of all shapes and sizes – to the less obvious, such as digital-camera card readers. The following pages show some of the most useful and desirable add-ons out there, but new ones come out all the time, so keep an eye on iPod news sites (see p.202). When it comes to purchasing, some accessories can be bought on the highstreet, but for the best selection and prices look online. Compare the offerings of the Apple Store, Amazon, eBay and others, or go straight to the manufacturers, many of which sell online. All the accessories we've listed below are compatible with third-generation iPods (those with a Dock-connector on the base). For older models and iPod Minis, check compatibility before purchasing.

extras

Voice recorders

Models include: Belkin Voice Recorder; Griffin iTalk
Cost (approx): $30–50/£25–40

Journalists, writers and thinkers who want to be able to record interviews or thoughts on the move will welcome the opportunity to turn their iPod into a Dictaphone capable of recording hundreds - even thousands – of hours of audio. Voice recorders let you do just this. They plug into the headphone jack, and usually also the remote-control connector, but a built-in speaker means that you don't have to unplug the device to hear what you've recorded. Once you're done, the sounds are saved as mono .WAV files, ready for transfer to a computer for storage, compressing, emailing or editing. No software or drivers are typically required, so you can literally just plug in and start recording.

A voice recorder with a speaker also allows you to use you iPod as a musical alarm clock – see p.162 – without having to plug it into a stereo.

Battery packs

Models include: Belkin Battery Pack
Cost (approx): $60/£40

If you don't find the iPod's eight
hours of battery life enough,
an external battery pack
will allow you to keep
the music playing
for longer. The
Belkin model pic-
tured attaches to the
Pod with non-scratch
suction cups and takes
four standard AA batter-
ies (enough for around
fifteen to twenty hours of
extra playing time).

Battery packs do exactly what they
say on the tin, but if you mainly use
your iPod in the car, you might find
it better value with an in-car power
cable (see p.177).

Or, if you don't mind kissing goodbye to your warranty, check out the
following page about making your
own battery pack from a playing-card
box, a FireWire socket, and a few
other bits and bobs you probably
don't have lying around:
http://drewperry.co.uk/
index.php?do=iPod&ipod=battery

extras

FM radio transmitters

Models include: Belkin TuneCast; Griffin iTrip; iRock Wireless FM Transmitter
Cost (approx): $40–60 (not available in the UK)

These cunning little devices turn an iPod into an extremely short-range FM radio station (many of them will also work with a computer or any other device with a headphone jack, though check before buying). Once you've attached a transmitter to your iPod, any radio within range (theoretically around 30 feet, though a few feet is more realistic to achieve decent sound) can then tune in to whatever the Pod is playing. The sound quality isn't quite as good as you'd get by attaching to a stereo via a cable (see p.120) and there can be interference, especially in cities. But they are very convenient and allow you to play through any FM radio, including those – such as portables and car stereos – which don't offer a line-in.

Of the models available at the time of writing, the iTrip (pictured) and iTrip Mini have the advantage of taking power directly from the Pod, so no batteries are required and there are no annoying cables. However, some users have complained of a weak signal compared to other models such as the Belkin TuneCast (which takes two AAA batteries or plugs into the mains or a car socket).

FM transmitters are currently legal in North America, but not in the UK, where they breach radio transmission laws. This doesn't seem to have stopped many Brits importing them from the States.

Cables & connections

Dock connector ▶ standard FireWire

Models include: SendStation PocketDock
Cost (approx): $20/£15

Turns the Dock connector of a third-
generation iPod into a standard 6-pin
FireWire socket, allowing you to
connect and recharge wherever you
find a FireWire cable. Not as useful as
a USB2/FireWire cable, perhaps, but
smaller to carry around.

Dock connector ▶ USB2 & FireWire

Models include: Apple USB2 cable
Cost (approx): $20/£15

If you use a third-generation iPod with a PC, you may already
have one of these. But they're also invaluable for Mac users who
want to be able to use their iPods as a portable hard drive to
move between Mac and older Windows machines (see p.156 for
more on this), since many of the latter don't have a FireWire port.

Headphone splitters

Models include: splitters by Monster and others
Cost (approx): $10/£7

Headphone splitters allow you to connect two pairs of headphones to a single
iPod (or any other personal stereo).

Wireless remote controls

Models include: TEN Technology naviPod
Cost (approx): $50/£35

If you (a) play your iPod through your hi-fi and (b) don't like getting out of your chair, you'll like the idea of an infrared iPod remote control. Obviously, it doesn't allow you to browse, but like the Apple wired remote the naviPod does let you access volume, play/pause and previous/next controls from anywhere in the room. Different models are available for iPods with or without Dock connections.

Wired remote control

Models include: Apple iPod Remote (included with some models)
Cost (approx): $40/£30 (including earphones)

For use on the go rather than in the home, Apple's own remote control – included with the more expensive iPod models – allows you access to the same basic controls from halfway up your (now longer) headphone cable. This saves you getting the iPod out of your pocket (and its case) every time you want to press Pause or

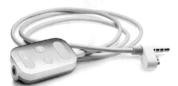

turn up the volume. A clip allows you to connect the remote to your pocket or collar for easy access, though the device is still a touch bulkier than would be ideal.

Docks & stands

Models include: **Apple iPod Dock**
Cost (approx): **$15–40/£10–30**

A "dock" allows you to quickly connect your iPod to a hi-fi, recharge it, and access the controls all at once. The hi-fi and power connections can be left permanently in place, so when you get home you simply drop your Pod in the dock and it's instantly connected. Most third-generation iPods have been sold with Apple's own Dock. If yours didn't come with one, they're available to buy separately.

Earlier iPods, however, don't have a Dock connector on the bottom, so the only equivalent Docks available – such as the BookEndz iPodDock – hold your iPod upside down, making the controls a bit hard to use. If you'd rather have your iPod the right way up, you could opt for a simple stand instead, such as Bubble Design's Habitat (pictured), which provides somewhere to put the Pod rather than any connections. Or try the Lego solution; see p.208.

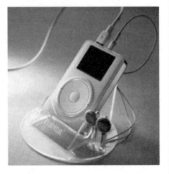

extras

Digital camera accessories

Models include: Belkin Media Reader; Belkin Digital Camera Link
Cost (approx): $90/£70

Most digital cameras store pictures on a small removable card. These tend to have a relatively small capacity of, say, 64 or 128 megabytes – plenty for most users, but not enough for serious photographers who want to take a large number of high-quality images without having to return home to their computer to download them. One option is to buy extra cards, but these are relatively expensive and low-capacity. Another option is to use an iPod – which has incomparably higher storage capacity – as a temporary home for your pictures. Belkin's Media Reader allows you to do this: attach it to your iPod's Dock connector (the device isn't compatible with older models) and you can download all your pictures to the iPod's hard drive, freeing up the card for reuse.

Belkin also make a device called Camera Link, which allows you to connect a mass-storage-class digital camera to the iPod via USB, instead of removing the card.

Car accessories

Chargers

Models include: cables by Belkin, Monster and others
Cost (approx): $10–20/£10–15

Connects an iPod to the power
(cigar-lighter) socket found in most
cars. Different models are available for
iPod's Dock/FireWire connectors.

Cassette adapters

Models include: adapters by Belkin, Sony and others
Cost (approx): $20/£10

Allows you to connect an iPod (or
any other device with a headphone
jack) to a car cassette player. You lose
a tiny bit of quality, but it's perfectly
good enough for car use.

Holsters

Models include: Belkin TuneDok; PodGear CarDock FM
Cost (approx): $25–60/£20–50

Connects an iPod to the power
(cigar-lighter) socket found in most
cars. Some are designed to be used
with a cassette adapter (see above),
while others – such as the PodGear
CarDock FM pictured – have a built-
in FM transmitter (see p.172).

Cases

There are hundreds of iPod cases available, from the waterproof (www.lilipods.com) and seriously protective "iPod Armor" (www.halfkeyboard.com) to the designer (www.gucci.com).

Second skins

Models include: iSkin; Speck Products Silicon Case
Cost (approx): $30/£20

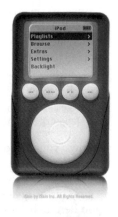

Stretchy iPod skins that do a good job of protecting your Pod from dust, scratches etc. They also offer a degree of shock-absorbence. They come in loads of colours and iSkin even offer an option of adding customized graphics to your model. It's worth checking to see whether the specific skin you want works with other accessories and the Dock.

iSkin by iSkin Inc. All Rights Reserved.

Sports cases

Models include: Marware Sportsuit Convertible
Cost (approx): $40/£35

There are loads of sports models on the market that feature either a wrist or armband as well as a standard belt clip, so you can go to the gym, jog, or whatever floats your boat. Marware's case also features an earphone pocket on the flap. Again, be sure that the case you buy doesn't compromise your ability to use the iPod with either the Dock or other accessories.

Earphones

The "earbuds" that come with both iPods and iPod Minis are OK for a while, but they're not exactly hi-fi and they do tend to get fried quite quickly. Also, there's the problem that when you wear them in the street everyone instantly knows what you've got in your pocket. There are thousands of alternatives you could consider (you'll find reviews of most of them at www.headphone.com), but the type that are really worth checking out – since you probably use your iPod when out and about in noisy surroundings – are sound-isolating in-ear headphones.

In-ear headphones

Models include: Shure E2c and E3c; Etymotic ER-series
Cost (approx): $100+/£70+

This kind of earphone sticks right into your ear canal and removes much ambient sound from the equation. Thus, you can listen to music at a much lower volume level, which is better for your ears and your iPod's battery. There are some relatively cheap models on the market, but if you can afford a bit more, check out the E2c and E3c models from Shure (a company who made their name manufacturing microphones). The isolation is impressive and the sound even more so. If you

have money to burn, another manufacturer worth investigating is Etymotic. Their ER-series headphones produce a stunning sound.

extras

iPod clothes & bags

Models include: SCOTTeVEST; Burton Ronin 2L; Felicidade Groove Bag
Cost (approx): $100/£75 and up

If listening to your Pod isn't enough, you could choose to wear it. If you don't mind forking out, there are various clothes and bags with built-in Pod capabilities, such as Burton's Ronin 2L snowboarding jacket, which features a set of duplicate iPod controls on the sleeve and a specially designed protective pouch. SCOTTeVEST

make many high-tech clothes, while Felicidade's Groove Bag is the best-known of the various bags with built-in speakers.

20

Extra
software

iPod and iTunes self-improvement

I f you've ever browsed a software download website and seen the amazing quantity of free and nearly free booty on offer, you won't be surprised to learn that there are scores of extra applications, utilities and plug-ins available for use with iTunes and the iPod. For once, there's more for Mac than PC, but Windows users will still find plenty on offer. We've spotlighted a few useful or interesting things in the next few pages, but there are loads more to be found throughout this book, and on the websites listed on p.201.

iPod to iTunes copying tools

Platform: Mac & PC
Cost: Shareware

There are a number of programs available that will let you copy music from your iPod to a computer — very useful if you want to restore your iTunes Library in the event of your computer dying or being stolen, or if you upgrade to a new machine.

You could also use one of these tools to share your music with friends using your iPod, though doing so with copyrighted music files between machines will push you onto the wrong side of the law.

iPod.iTunes and iPodRip will both do the job on a Mac, while EphPod is a good choice for PC users. Also worth exploring, and available for both Mac and PC, is PodUtil.

iPod.iTunes www.crispsofties.com
iPodRip www.thelittleappfactory.com
EphPod www.ephpod.com
PodUtil www.kennettnet.co.uk/software

These kind of applications can also help you perform other syncing tasks with an iPod and iTunes, though bear in mind that they sometimes stop working when you install a new version of iTunes or update your iPod's software.

iTunes controllers

Platform: **Mac**
Cost: **Shareware**

iTunes controller applications come in many forms and with loads of different features: floating windows, hotkeys, alarm clocks, menu-bar controls, etc. A couple worth checking out are M-Beat (www.thelittleappfactory.com) and MenuTunes (www.ithinksw.com). At the time of writing, all the decent ones out there are for the Mac; search the download archives listed on p.201 for more controller programs.

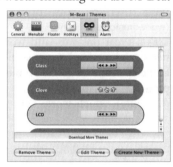

AppleScripts

Platform: **Mac**
Cost: **Freeware**

AppleScript is a simple programming language that can be used to automate tasks and functions on a Mac. Hundreds have been written for iTunes and iPods; they can do everything from automatically downloading cover art for tracks in your Library, to making it possible to delete song files from within a playlist. There are loads online, though you won't find a better selection than those offered by Doug:

Doug's AppleScripts www.malcolmadams.com/itunes

extras

Musicmatch

Platform: PC
Cost: Free

If you really don't get on with iTunes and aren't that bothered about accessing the iTunes Music Store there are loads of other jukebox programs available. But if you want to an alternative iPod interface, your only realistic choice is Musicmatch (www.musicmatch.com).

It's a great program and works well with a Pod, though you need to download a special plug-in to get the ball rolling (it's available from both the Apple and Musicmatch websites). The program also integrates with a Musicmatch Downloads store (US only), which works very similarly to Apple's.

iPod icons

Platform: Mac (some PC available)
Cost: Free

OK, they're not exactly extra programs, but anyone who wants to turn their computer into an iPod shrine might be interested in the free icon families – including many devoted to iPods – available from Xicons (www.xicons.com). The PC selection (click XP in the top corner) is still relatively small, but growing each week.

On a Mac, click an icon family and it will automatically start to download, unstuffing once complete. Locate the unstuffed folder, choose an icon, single-click it and press Apple+C for copy. Then select the file on which you want to use the icon and press Apple+I to bring up the Show Info box.

Click the current icon at the top of the box and press Apple+V (paste) to overwrite it with the new one (you can also get rid of it later by clicking it here and pressing backspace).

If you can't find a Mac icon that does your Pod justice, download Pic2Icon (www.sugarcubesoftware.com) and make your own.

And more...

iEatBrainz http://homepage.com/jbtule Cost: Free
Uses the "sound" of a song to search for its artist details within the MusicBrainz online database. Useful if Gracenote fails you.

Ear Mail www.newton-eig.com Cost: $50
Listen to your emails on your iPod.

webRemote www.deadendsw.com Cost: Shareware
Control iTunes using any Web browser.

PodQuest www.mibasoft.dk Cost: $10
Download MapQuest driving instructions to your iPod.

Fetch Art http://staff.washington.edu/yoel/fetchart Cost: Free
Automatically download album artwork from Amazon.

LED Spectrum Analyser www.maczoop.com Cost: Shareware
Fully featured visualizer program that emulates a spectrum analyser.

ListSaver www.deadendsw.com Cost: Shareware
Back up and restore iTunes playlists.

DotPod www.dotpod.net Cost: Shareware
Make music available over the Internet from your iPod (only legal with uncopyrighted music).

iBrew www.dropcap.co.uk/ibrew Cost: Free
Allows your iPod to connect with a regular teapot to test the strength and temperature of your cuppa-to-be.

HELP &
MAINTENANCE

21
Backing up
keeping your music safe

Just like any other computer file, music files can be deleted or damaged. Hard drives die, and computers get stolen, damaged or destroyed. As we've seen (see p.182), with the right software it's perfectly possible to recover music from your iPod back to your computer. However, if you have more music on your computer than your Pod, or if you regularly carry your laptop and Pod around in the same bag, it's definitely worth having a back-up copy of your archive.

Backing up iTunes files

There's no point in simply copying files to a separate folder on your hard drive, or even a separate partition, because if your computer is stolen or the drive damaged, you loose both your original and backup copy. Equally a second internal drive is of little use if your machine goes walkies. For a backup to be useful it needs to be housed on some kind of external media, either optical disc (CD or DVD), an external hard drive, or perhaps even online with a remote server.

And backing up iTunes properly is not simply a matter of duplicating the actual song files: you need to create a copy of the whole iTunes folder (found in your Home folder's "Music folder" on a Mac and in "My Music" on a PC), which contains not only the songs but also a record of all your playlists, preferences, etc, in two databases, named "iTunes Music Library.xml" and "iTunes 4 Music Library".

Backing up to an external drive

The most convenient way to back up your iTunes folder is to drag a copy to an external drive that can be kept completely separate from your computer. Such drives are relatively cheap (considering how much woe they can save you from), are very easy to use, and are more than capacious enough to do the job. With an external hard drive you can copy everything in one

Consolidate Library...

By selecting "Consolidate Library" from the iTunes Advanced menu, iTunes scans your whole system for music files and then copies them all to your Library. You could then search for and delete the originals using either your OS X or Windows search functions. This is a very useful exercise to perform prior to moving your Library to a new machine or backing it up to an external drive (see above).

go and, should the worst happen, restoring your iTunes folder is easy.

First, open Preferences and in the Advanced pane tick both the check boxes that relate to the iTunes folder, then quit iTunes and drag the whole back-up iTunes folder from the hard drive to its original location; if you need to replace an existing iTunes folder in that location, do so. Now relaunch iTunes and your library, playlists and preferences will have been recreated.

Backing up to DVD or CD

If you don't want to buy an external hard drive but already have either a CD or DVD burner, then you can use this as a means of backing up your song files. CDs are not ideal, because of their relatively small capacity, but DVDs are great (you should be able to fit the equivalent of around 150 audio CDs on a single DVDR).

First, create a new playlist and drag your Library icon (or whatever you want to back up) onto it in the Source list. Next, open Preferences and under Burning choose to create a data DVD (or CD). Close Preferences, select the playlist, and hit the Burn button in the top right of the iTunes window. Assuming your Library is pretty large, iTunes will not be able to fit all the songs on a single disc. When iTunes has burned what it can to the first disc, it will prompt you to insert subsequent discs until the job is done.

To restore these song files, drag them from the optical discs into the open iTunes window, which will prompt iTunes to copy them to the iTunes music folder.

Back up with Backup

OS X users who sign up for a .Mac account gain access to an Apple program called Backup, which can be used to copy your files to either an optical disc, external hard drive or remote server (.Mac also provides you with an online backup drive called iDisk). For more details, see www.mac.com

> ▶ **TIP:** You will additionally need to locate your
> iTunes Library file and back it up separately in
> order to save your playlists. It is easily
> restored by simply dragging the backup copy into the
> iTunes folder.

Incremental backups

A backup is only useful if it is done regularly. If you are using an external hard drive simple copy the iTunes folder onto the drive once every few weeks or so and replace the backed-up one, alternatively use a third party application (see below) to synchronize your iTunes folder and the external drive's version.

If you are using the burning-playlists method, here's a little trick to help you keep track of what's changed in your Library in the time since your last backup. Create a new Smart Playlist (see p.65) that only features songs added after the date that you backed up. When you next feel the need to create a backup DVD, simply burn this Smart Playlist and then change its perameters to only feature songs added from that date.

Utilities

Check the software archives listed on p.204 for backing-up utilities, or go straight to Anapod:

Anapod www.redchairsoftware.com/anapod/ctable.php

22

iTunes & iPod troubleshooting

help!

espite the minimalist design of the iPod, and the intuitive look and feel of iTunes, both can throw the occasional curve ball. There are a million and one things that might be the cause of your woes – and we simply don't have the room in a book of this size to cover all of them. However, this chapter does address many of the most common problems, and provides some troubleshooting tips to help you get your Pod and computer back on track. As for the rest, there's always the Internet, so if we don't help you here turn to p.203 for a list of online resources.

iPod worries

Just like regular computers, iPods sometimes crash, freeze up, or generally just start behaving like belligerent two-year-olds. When this happens you can generally solve the problem by resetting your Pod (see box), just like you might reboot a computer. This is generally the fault of a software glitch. But if the problem is down to your hard drive...

Disk scan

If your iPod suspects that there might be an issue with its hard drive, it will automatically start to run its in-built disk scan utility. The screen will display a disk and magnifying glass icon while the scan is in process (which can take around twenty minutes). When the scan is complete, you will be presented with an icon.

▶ **Everything's OK** You have nothing to worry about – your hard drive is in perfect condition.

▶ **Scan failed** The scan has failed and will be repeated next time you turn on your iPod.

▶ **Scan found issues** The scan has found problems on your hard drive, but repaired them. If you see this icon you need to restore your iPod using an iPod Software Updater (see p.156), downloadable from the Apple website.

▶ **Sad iPod icon** This is not good – it means your iPod should be sent away to be repaired.

Resetting an iPod

Resetting an iPod
Step 1. Connect the iPod to its power supply.
Step 2. Toggle the Hold switch on and then off again.
Step 3. Press and hold the ▶ II and **Menu** buttons for around six seconds until the Apple logo appears.

Resetting an iPod Mini
Step 1. Connect the iPod Mini to its power supply.
Step 2. Toggle the Hold switch on and then off again.
Step 3. Press and hold the **Menu** and **Select** buttons for around six seconds until the Apple logo appears.

My iPod won't mount or dismount

If your computer refuses to mount or dismount your iPod as a FireWire drive, even though Disk Use is enabled (see p.155), try forcing it: reset the Pod (see box above) and, at the Apple logo screen, either press and hold ◄◄ and ▶▶ on an iPod, or press and hold **Select** and ▶ II on an iPod Mini.

Battery problems

There has been much controversy about the life span of the iPod battery (see p.13) and the speed with which it runs down when being used. Here are a few things that you can do on a

TIP: If you want to run various other tests on your iPod, enter Diagnostic Mode. Reset your iPod (see box) and at the Apple logo screen press ◄◄, ▶▶ and **Select** until you hear a little chirp and a new menu appears. These tests are quite techie, so be sure you know what you are doing before you start. For more, see www.ipoding.com/prev/001.html

day-to-day basis to maximize the listening time you get from a single battery charge.

▶ Make sure you're not running an old iPod software version (see p.36).

▶ Buy a decent pair of "sound isolating" headphones (see p.179), you won't have to listen to your music at such high volume.

▶ Avoid using the backlight, and turn off the clock and calendar alarm functions. While you're at it, turn the iPod's Ticker off.

▶ Use lower-quality song files (see p.106) – the iPod doesn't have to work so hard to play them. And try not to use the ◀◀ and ▶▶ buttons too frequently, as they require more hard-drive use.

▶ Use the Hold switch so that your iPod doesn't sing to itself in your pocket when buttons get pressed accidentally. And turn off Repeat mode.

If your iPod battery does eventually run out of steam either: send the Pod to Apple for a replacement (this will be free if your warranty hasn't expired); get a company such as iPodResQ or PlugStore to come to your aid; or do it yourself, by buying a new battery and downloading instructions from a company such as iPod Mini Batteries (not just for iPod Minis!) or iPod Battery.com.

Service & Support www.apple.com/support/ipod
iPodBattery.com www.ipodbattery.com (US)
iPodResQ www.ipodresq.com (US)
iPod Mini Batteries www.ipodminibattery.com (UK)
PlugStore www.plugstore.net (UK)

The display is in the wrong language

Follow these steps to get back to English:

▶ Hit the Menu button a few times to reach the top-level menu.

▶ Select the third item from the bottom – always Settings.

▶ Again, select the third item (the Language menu) and find English.

iTunes worries

For iTunes troubleshooting advice relating to burning CDs and DVDs, see p.87. And for problems playing music, see p.78. Here are a few other problems that you may encounter.

I've run out of disk space on my computer

First of all, clean up your iTunes Library. Sort it by file size (see p.84) and either delete any unwanted uncompressed files (AIFFs or WAVs) or convert them to something more space efficient (see p.104). Next look at your system as a whole and see if you can save any space by deleting, or archiving, old files and disposing of temporary files. Finally, consider getting an extra hard drive (see p.9).

iTunes says my Library file is invalid

Within every iTunes folder, along with the actual music folders, you should also find an iTunes Library file. This contains a database of information that points iTunes to your music files and records playlists, play counts and more.

If your Library file seems to be missing or corrupt, you could simply restore the file, if you ever backed it up (see p.189). Or you could use a program like iPodRip (see p.182) to restore the information from your iPod to iTunes. Finally, you could simply drag your iTunes Music folder (located inside the iTunes folder

Dead computers, new computers

If your computer dies or gets stolen, you can – once you have a new one – either restore your music archive from a backup, if you made one (see p.189), or download a program that lets you copy the music from your iPod to your computer (see p.182, but don't sync your iPod with the new computer's empty iTunes Library!). If you upgrade your computer, the same options apply.

in your Music folder on a Mac and in My Music on a PC) to the Library icon in iTune's Source list. This should bring back all the songs, but not playlists, playcounts and other information.

You may also run in to this kind of problem if you've moved your music archive to somewhere other than the default location. In this case, point iTunes to the new location via the Advanced tab in Preferences.

The text in my song list looks garbled

This is most likely caused by problems with your ID3 tags (special bits of code within music files that record the track information that you see when you are browsing your iTunes Library). The problem is easily solved: in the song list, select the tracks causing you grief and choose "Convert ID3 Tags…" from the iTunes Advanced menu.

Still struggling?

Try upgrading to the most up-to-date version of iTunes (see p.36) or, if you are already up-to-date, try reinstalling. But, if at all possible, back up first.

> ▶ For more iPod and iTunes troubleshooting advice, search for an answer online. Google (including http://groups.google.com) is a great places to start, but also try Apple's own Net discussion area (http://discussions.info.apple.com) and the iPod supersites listed on p.202.

iPODOLOGY

23

iPods online

online resources and forums

I f you want to find out more about any of the subjects covered in this book – or you want to track down that illusive iPod accessory, join a forum or download the latest iTunes plug-ins – you're going to have to hit the Web. There's an almost frightening number of iPod and iTunes sites out there, including comprehensive Pod portals, with discussion forums, troubleshooting tips, news and reviews. Apple's own site is also a useful resource. Following are some of the best and most useful. For more, try searching Google.

iPod sites and forums

Everything iPod www.everythingipod.com
iPoding www.ipoding.com
iPods-Mini-iPods www.ipods-mini-ipod.com
iPodLounge www.ipodlounge.com
iPod Studio http://ipodstudio.com

Apple

Home www.apple.com
iTunes/iPod home www.apple.com/music
Apple Store www.apple.com/store
Apple Discussions http://discussions.info.apple.com
Software Updates www.apple.com/support/downloads
Service & Support www.apple.com/support/ipod

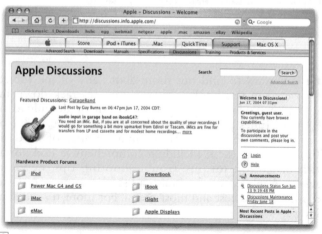

Help and maintenance

Apple www.info.apple.com/usen/ipod/tshoot.html
Chipmunk www.chipmunk.nl/iPod
iPod Hacks www.ipodhacks.com
MacFixit www.macfixit.com

Buying and accessories

Amazon www.amazon.com
Apple Store www.apple.com/store
Everything iPod www.everythingipod.com
Griffin www.griffintechnology.com
iPodLounge www.ipodlounge.com/loungestore.php

iPodology

Downloads

About http://macs.about.com/cs/itunes/a/itunes_utils.htm
Doug's AppleScripts www.malcolmadams.com/itunes
iPodLounge www.ipodlounge.com/downloads.php
iPodSoft www.ipodsoft.com
LittleAppFactory www.thelittleappfactory.com
TuCows www.tucows.com

iPod blogs

BlogFreaks http://ipod.blogfreaks.com
iPod News www.ipod-news.blogspot.com
MyiPodBlog http://myipodblog.blospot.com
The iPod Blog www.theipodblog.com

iPod history

Design Chain www.designchain.com/coverstory.asp?issue=summer02
Wikipedia http://en.wikipedia.org/wiki/IPod

> **TIP: If you have a suggestion about how the
> iPod could be improved, tell Apple, at:
> www.apple.com/feedback/ipod.html**

24
iPodd

stranger than fiction

It is, without a doubt, a crazy world, and there's nothing quite like music, gadgets and fads to bring the crackpots out of the cupboard. What follows are a few dispatches from the people who put the odd in the Pod.

Engravings from hell

What not to get engraved on your little shiny friend:
www.ipodlaughs.com/ipod/iengraver
www.methodshop.com/mp3/articles/ipodengraving/index.stm
www.ipodlaughs.com/ipod/ipocalypse/disturbingengravings.asp

And, if you want the T-shirt, visit…
www.cafeshops.com/ipod_laughs

Linux on iPod

Bored of playing music? Why not use your iPod as a platform
for a UNIX-based operating system?

Linux on iPod - Screenshots

The following images are photos taken of the kernel startup messages.

Home
Screen Shots
Documentation
Download
Forums
Support & Help
Project Sponsors
FAQ's
Legal
Linux on iPod at
SourceForge.

Make a Donation

Animations

Apple-ad-meets-Microsoft-man magic moment...
www.macboy.com/cartoons/ballmer

Photo galleries

What do you get if you cross an iPod with PhotoShop...?
www.ipodlaughs.com/ipod/ipocalypse

And for shots of globetrotting Pods...
http://gallery.ipodlounge.com

What do you think – hoax, or the best idea since sliced bread?

iShave
Rocken Sie nicht unrasiert!

Hochkarätige Schertechnologie

Ein Y-geometrischer Scherkopf garantiert eine glatte und hautfreundliche Rasur. Kombiniert mit dem hochwertigen Scherkopf-Schwingsystem erfasst der iShave durch das 6-fach System mehr Barthaare in weniger Zügen, d.h. sie haben noch vor Ende des Liedes eine glatte und sanft rasierte Haut.

iGod

And if you want to read the Bible whilst listening to your favourite music, you're going to need this:

BiblePod
http://biblepod.kainjow.com

Bricking it

Who needs a Dock when all the raw materials are sitting at the back of the toy cupboard?

www.pitt.edu/~jas2377
/lego_tutorial

In fact, who needs an iPod at all when you have Lego?

Here's one Pete made earlier...

> **TIP:** If you don't like the backlight colour of your iPod's screen and buttons – and you don't mind voiding your warranty – try something in blue, green or orange. Visit www.ipodmods.com and check out their full customization service.

INDEX

Index

◀ index